POLYNYA

Library and Archives Canada Cataloguing in Publication

Vincelette, Mélanie, 1975-
[Polynie. English]
    Polynya / Mélanie Vincelette.

Translation of: Polynie.
Translated by Donald Winkler and Sheila Fischman.
Issued in print and electronic formats.
ISBN 978-1-77161-201-2 (paperback).--ISBN 978-1-77161-202-9 (html).--ISBN 978-1-77161-203-6 (pdf)

I. Fischman, Sheila, translator II. Winkler, Donald, translator
III.Title. IV. Title: Polynie. English

PS8593.I4457P6413 2016   C813'.6   C2016-906166-3
                                    C2016-906167-1

Published by Mosaic Press, Oakville, Ontario, Canada, 2016.

MOSAIC PRESS, Publishers

Copyright © 2011 Éditions Robert Laffont

Translation Copyright © 2016 Sheila Fischman and Donald Winkler

Printed and Bound in Canada

Designed by Courtney Blok

ONTARIO ARTS COUNCIL
CONSEIL DES ARTS DE L'ONTARIO
an Ontario government agency
un organisme du gouvernement de l'Ontario

We acknowledge the Ontario Arts Council
for their support of our publishing program
We acknowledge the Ontario Media Development Corporation
for their support of our publishing program

Funded by the   Financé par le
Government   gouvernement
of Canada   du Canada

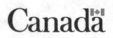

MOSAIC PRESS
1252 Speers Road, Units 1 & 2
Oakville, Ontario L6L 5N9
phone: (905) 825-2130

info@mosaic-press.com

POLYNYA

MÉLANIE
VINCELETTE

Translated from the French
by Sheila Fischman and Donald Winkler

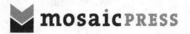 mosaicPRESS

Other Works by Mélanie Vincelette

Petites géographies orientales, 2001

Qui a tué magellan? Et autres nouvelles, 2004

Crimes horticoles, 2006

Respect yourself

Inuit sentence

1
Puffball

Baffin Island. May 3. The Canadian Arctic Archipelago.

"The Chinese discovered America." Those were the words scribbled in ink on the forearm of my brother Rosaire, found dead on election day by Lumi, the star stripper at the Arctic Circle Hotel. When she opened the door of Room 7 to the police, she was naked under her parka and held in both hands a Styrofoam cup filled with boiling hot tea, on which her lipstick had imprinted a kiss. Lumi, who was trying to hold the parka shut over her bronzed body, didn't seem too upset. Under the white fur hood, her gray-green eyes and her heart-shaped mouth discouraged the police, for a few minutes, from suspecting they might be in the presence of a murderer.

Iqaluit, the village where the Arctic Circle can be found, is the Las Vegas of the Far North. There you play bingo and hang out at the bars. The Arctic Circle is known for its arctic char pizza. Tourists bring it back boxed in their luggage. For his last meal, Rosaire seemed to have swallowed little puffballs in brown butter eaten straight from a cast-iron frying pan found in the kitchenette. In the bathtub there was hydroponic alfalfa that he grew on the assumption that the sprouts would keep him from growing old. Baffin Island's where Rosaire Nicolet found happiness before facing death. I'm guilty of one thing only: of having envied him, because his life was always what he imagined it to be every night in his dreams.

My brother was a lawyer in international law. He was one of a committee of experts whose mandate was to prove that the Canadian continental plateau is linked to the Lomonosov Ridge, a chain of underwater mountains. The Lomonosov Ridge will one day determine who owns the Arctic's deep sea wealth. Denmark, Russia, and Canada are arguing over that sovereignty. The Russians even planted their flag there with a mini-submarine. In the past, Rosaire had also helped out the Inuit with their territorial demands, especially when Nunavut was created. On the day of his death, he was dressed Caribbean style and wore a white linen jacket trimmed in blue braid with a nautical escutcheon on the front, madras Bermudas, and leather moccasins with no socks. His blond hair was bleached by sea salt, his complexion was dark, and his lips pale pink, almost white. Blotches of calamine lotion spotted his jawbone where there was a two-day beard. His watch had stopped at 11:11. Under the bed there was a peach pit in a piece of plastic wrap. I was stunned. It all seemed so weird.

Lumi had whispered just one thing to the police when she'd called for help: "I don't know how to do CPR. Do I pinch his nostrils and then blow into his mouth?"

Cargo ships, airplanes, and entire civilizations vanish into the Arctic on a regular basis, leaving only rumours and unanswered questions in the milky whiteness of their wake. At least we knew that Rosaire had not been swallowed up by a humpback whale and that he hadn't fallen through the ice, theories often rolled out to explain the disappearance of Arctic explorers. Solving a murder in this tiny hermetically sealed community would turn out to be harder than expected, even if it was almost impossible to get off Baffin Island. The longest road was only seventy kilometres long, stopping short at an enormous glacier seventy-five metres high.

2

The Dangers of Scarlet Fever

When Rosaire died I was working as a cook at a small gold mine two days from Iqaluit by dog sled. When I was hired, they asked me if I was up to preparing whale and muskox. I love being a cook. The work has always made my life easy. I'm not someone who can fathom people who waste their lives doing work they hate. But when I was taken on at the mine I had no idea that I'd meet the woman I would love forever, or that I would witness unspeakable crimes. Since the end of winter I'd hoped for only one thing: that one day we'd be struck by lightning, Marcelline and I, in the root cellar.

I was scaling the sooty skin of an arctic char to get at the pink flesh when I learned about my brother's death. I can still see Marcelline, the beautiful glaciologist, her eyes blue with sadness, standing between the double doors, having just learned what was about to change my life.

"Ambroise, something terrible has happened at Iqaluit. Rosaire won't be coming to see us tonight. Rosaire is dead. Lumi found him in his room at the Arctic Circle. The police think they had a fight."

Marcelline had spoken softly, coming towards me as if she wanted to bury her face in the collar of my chef's coat, far too white.

"What? That's impossible! Gone to heaven?" I mumbled, incredulous.

"Yes, Ambroise. God has called him," she said, her voice breaking.

An Inuit throat song welled up in me, like a requiem murmured by children. I didn't answer, mesmerized by the perfect symmetry of Marcelline's face. I hadn't really absorbed what she'd just said. Most of the time, when she looked me in the eyes, I went deaf. So I went on filleting the salmony flesh and shot a glance towards the winterized window with its double layer of clear plastic. Outside, a white fox was burrowing under the garbage container where there were three cubs. The little family seemed to have decided to live off our leavings rather than hunt, as though it had won the lottery.

I was not far from giving up the ghost. I'd been close to my brother, our bond was unbreakable. Without Rosaire, my life had no shape. It was as if I'd just spent the night outside, totally naked. I had hypothermia. My temperature had dropped two degrees, I had goosebumps, and all my body hair was standing on end, giving me an extra layer of insulation. I was breathing with difficulty, as though I had steel lungs. I'd lost all feeling in my hands and my filleting knife bounced off my boot. I fainted like a young actress the night of her premiere, and my 6' 4" body remained motionless on the ground. I'd always had a paraffin complexion, but I must have been as white as a doe's belly. I lay on the floor covered with pages from the *Baffin Daily News*. On the front page, you could read: *Even though the Rochemelon Glacier between France and Italy in the Alps will disappear if the climate heats up another three degrees, some politicians visiting Iqaluit refuse to admit that the temperature is rising, saying only that on December 26, 1803, lettuce was harvested in Montreal, and that on May 10, 2009, on Mother's Day, it snowed.*

Marcelline crouched down beside me and took me in her arms and I felt her lips on my earlobe.

"Ambroise, your pupils are dilated. Lumi's being questioned right now in Iqaluit. They think she's guilty. They found a strange sentence written on your brother's arm: 'The Chinese discovered America.'"

"Did they steal our map? The map of our ancestor, Jean Nicolet?" I mumbled weakly.

Lumi had taken full advantage of the touristic and economic boom in the Arctic, made possible because of climate change and the retreat of the glaciers. She was a stripper in the famous Arctic Circle Hotel bar, where you could admire the biggest stuffed polar bear head in North America. The strippers there wore scouts' mini-shorts and work boots, and made their entrances sitting on a trapeze. In the air foggy with contraband tobacco, you could make out a mix of snowmobile fuel and shea butter.

Marie-Perle, who had briefly hung out with Rosaire and who also worked at the Arctic Circle, told the local paper that she was sure Lumi was the sole perpetrator of the murder. She'd seen her in a fight with Rosaire the day before, in the women's toilets that also served as dressing rooms. It was a savage battle, in the course of which they'd smashed two of the seventy-two fluorescent tubes on the tanning bed that afforded a bit of light therapy during the long polar nights. Marie-Perle, a mini-tart with hair as transparent as fishing line, had a tiny baby seal tattooed on the small of her back. In the photo that came with the article she had a hand curled under her chin, nails manicured, and was visibly thrilled at the thought of one day becoming the star stripper at the most popular bar on Baffin Island, a place where the waitresses wore miniskirts depicting the British flag, and where several dancers' backs sported scarlet fever scars. These women wanted to please at any cost, so they could get big tips. They played with emotions and received money in exchange. They winked with their coal black lashes and tittered at each remark so that the men would feel droll and important. At the Arctic Circle they forgot their foremen even existed, and drowned their lives as drillers in shots of *eau-de-vie*. "When Lumi says something, you can taste it in your mouth," Rosaire had confessed to me. "If I'm hungry, I ask her to pronounce 'strawberry charlotte.'"

Lumi, like all the other strippers, gave the mechanics, machinists and electricians injections of confidence with stolen kisses. That year she had promised three men, including my brother Rosaire and a young soldier, that she would marry them. In a way, that was part of her job. She sold each one the idea that he was unique. She made him believe that he was getting special treatment, that she loved him for real, but that she didn't have enough money to leave this awful life. That's how she had three suitors at the same time and could ask for a New Year's gift to mark their engagement in a singular way: not with a ring or a diamond solitaire but with an insurance policy for which she would be the sole beneficiary. That didn't mean she had it in her to be a murderer. But rumours circulated in Iqaluit that she was on the Russians' payroll and that she cozied up to naïve young soldiers to worm state secrets out of them.

Polynya

The more populations are isolated, the more fanciful the rumours they generate. Rosaire, during his negotiations with the Inuit chiefs, was suspected of collusion with Brice de Saxe Majolique, the eccentric owner of the gold mine. Lumi was good at what she did, she had an excellent reputation, and had always said that she worked so that one day she could complete her university education. It just so happened that Rosaire, who was one of her three fiancés, was found dead in her hotel room. And Lumi was primed to cash in an insurance policy of more than a million dollars. North of the sixtieth parallel though, things can go bad in a flash.

It was Marcelline who brought me back to life. Standing in the kitchen, numbly shoving a loaf of salt herb bread into the oven, my work boots on the *Baffin Daily News*, I thought about that sentence scrawled on my brother's forearm: "The Chinese discovered America." It was an obvious reference to our medieval *mappemonde*, the reproduction of a Chinese map dating from 1418. That map could mean that world history, as conceived for centuries by esteemed historians, had to be rewritten.

The first hours of grieving are strange. I was positive that Rosaire hadn't died, that he was hiding out on a Caribbean island for reasons yet to be revealed. Weighed down by grief, the human soul will take the most luminous detours to ward off intolerable facts. I could not accept what had happened.

3

The Gold Digger

My name is Ambroise Nicolet, and I lost my brother Rosaire in the Canadian Arctic Archipelago. That same night, all the mine employees gathered on the shore to see the first school of belugas silently entering the bay. Marcelline stayed behind with me in the kitchen, because there was no way for me to instantly leave the mine. I cooked her "angry capelins," fish you make bite their own tails before plunging them into the fat.

"I was brought up in an ice fishing supply station, the famous white fishery. Angry capelins, that was Rosaire's favourite dish. You like it?"

"Yes, I love it. You're really inspired when it comes to local food."

"Before, at this time of year, there was Arctic cod in Hudson's Bay. Now the schools have been replaced by capelins, they're a lot smaller."

"So the bears are going to be hungry this year."

"Rosaire always used to say that life keeps changing. That you had to know how to adapt. He said it was guaranteed that you'd never stay bored for long. He insisted that I underestimated my desire for change, but that the universe would take care of things for me, strewing my path with lessons I could never have foreseen."

"Rosaire's death must be one of them."

As she murmured those words, Marcelline's putty-coloured eyes welled up with compassion. I decided to tell her about one of my vivid memories of Rosaire, our little vendetta.

"When I was twelve years old I shot a cherry with a peashooter at Rosaire's eye, and almost blinded him on one side. The eye snapped shut immediately, like a flesh-eating plant. It turned purple and swelled up like an eggplant. Right then I knew I was going to need a way to survive. To survive Rosaire and the violent vendetta he'd be planning. I fended off his silent war by looking over my shoulder every fifteen minutes for three and a half months. When he finally got his chance, his revenge was brutal. In a moment of "panic," as he described it, he grabbed a shotgun from the wall that our father used to kill rabbits, and shot me at close range as I ran towards the woods. I was hit once in the behind but I never complained to our mother, afraid that she'd punish both of us within an inch of our lives."

"Your brother shot you and you didn't tell anybody? At that age you're usually so spiteful that you'll blame your brother any chance you get."

"The worst is that I've kept the secret, and I've had this lead shot in my rear ever since. The wound healed, but sometimes I think about having it taken out."

Marcelline could hardly keep from laughing. I kept going.

"I know Rosaire felt very guilty. I never told him that I held it against him. And it didn't take me long to forgive him. When a woman touches my butt and the lead shot and asks me about the strange little pea under the surface of my skin, I sometimes feel I gave in too soon. I didn't know how to defend myself against my brother. Rosaire was always better looking, more intelligent, more at ease socially than I was. Now that he's not there anymore I'll keep this shot inside me forever in memory of our childhood."

"You'll never have it taken out?"

"I never talked to Rosaire about it. I wouldn't have wanted him to worry about me for anything in the world. My silence was my forgiveness."

That night in the cafeteria, with the lights out, we talked nonstop, Marcelline and I. I explained how important Rosaire was to me. How our fraternal bond had for a long time been my means of survival. Nothing was difficult in his royal, noble, infinite presence. Loves were changeable and brief, but my brother was, and always would be, there when life turned its back on me. With him, I had a bond that was close to scriptural. He was the only one who knew everything.

I never thought that one day I was going to have to learn how to live without him. I also found it hard to believe what Marie-Perle, the gold digger, said. Lumi could not have killed him.

4

The Skunk from Montana

Our ancestor, the explorer Jean Nicolet, travelled up the Saint Lawrence in 1642 to the Great Lakes, as vast as seas. He wore a Ming robe embroidered with peacock feather threads, in floral motifs the colour of coral. Intoxicated by Marco Polo's tales, Jean Nicolet thought he was arriving in a land brimming with curiosities. He was going to eat rhubarb jam in blue porcelain bowls served by a young girl with almond eyes, dressed in raw silk, with oil-smooth hair tied up in a long braid. Jean Nicolet sported an outfit worthy of the mandarins he expected to meet. His armada of fifty Huron canoes loaded with furs made its way up the Saint Lawrence Valley going westward. He had in his possession a strange map, a reproduction of a *mappemonde* from 1418 showing that the Chinese had explored the coasts of the New World long before Columbus. There was even a route leading to the Arctic continent on the back of it, drawn freehand in a thick indigo line. A map that would later be declared to have been drawn up and dated by a forger.

One of the first places where Jean Nicolet stopped became a city today called Lachine. Like many explorers after Columbus, Jean Nicolet only had one thought in mind: to find the celestial empire.

In the cafeteria I was seated across from Marcelline, who hadn't eaten a single angry capelin. She asked me why someone had written that strange sentence on my brother's arm.

"Rosaire found the archives of our ancestor, Jean Nicolet, in our father's attic, along with an old world map that would change our lives. I couldn't imagine that it was also going to play a role in Rosaire's death."

Why did someone kill Rosaire? "The Chinese discovered America." I couldn't get the story straight in my head. What did that sentence on his forearm mean?

I was baffled, and said so to Marcelline.

On the summer Sundays of our childhood, we used to rummage through boxes in the attic that held the family archives. Rosaire had found there a notebook full of photos and anecdotes. It had belonged to our late uncle, who had travelled to the West on the trail of his ancestor. In those pages, he recounted that Jean Nicolet had arrived in an Amerindian community that had become rich thanks to the fur trade and its many exchanges with Europeans. He had entered a deciduous forest with mirrors hanging from the leaves. It was the native people who had placed them there, having received them in exchange for ermine, beaver and wolf skins. In this forest of precious mirrors graced with gold leaf, you saw your reflection multiplied a thousand times in glass sometimes convex, sometimes bevelled, whose silvering had often been altered by the weather. Jean Nicolet's life enchanted me. His tales gave me a taste for adventure, the desire to take the measure of unknown worlds. My cage had sprung open.

While Rosaire went to university, I chose to take small jobs. Before becoming a cook in the Canadian Arctic Archipelago, I drove an eighteen-wheeler on the ice roads of the far north. My timidity stood in the way of my seeking out women looking for casual lovers among seasonal workers. My brother paid me a visit at Christmas, to give himself a break. I always had more luck with women when he was there. He attracted them like a magnet. He was a lousy dancer, but he danced every night. He loved to sing karaoke and he casually played, one-handed, a drum made of sea lion guts, making off with all the prizes. Even his amputated finger gave him an aura of mystery that had the women whispering among themselves. He knew how to talk about wines with a poetry that drew sighs from the ladies. "This late harvest wine has an aroma of raisins, liquid gold and earthy moss." The girls' eyes lit up.

He wore a ridiculous hat of fleece-lined polecat fur that the women loved to stroke. It was literally as if he had a skunk on his head, its long, white-striped black tail falling onto his neck. Even with this preposterous headgear he was irresistible, as he inspired in women an unshakeable confidence. They approached him and caressed the animal's tail; he would say: "It's a skunk from Montana, I killed it myself." He had not yet understood that there was nothing very virile about killing a polecat in a northern setting where the sun rises, then sets an hour later. Here one hunted whales in teams of six.

My brother had just turned thirty-five.

5

Polar Love

When I think of Marcelline, I have in mind the Fibonacci series, where each number in the mathematical formula is the sum of the two that precede it. We find its applications in the spiral form of shells, sunflowers, pineapples and pine cones. Perfection. I heard Rosaire ask the mine pastor if the Anglican Church - Saint Jude of Iqualuit, in the Arctic diocese, destroyed by fire and rebuilt in big cement blocks painted white - respected the rules of this sequence, given its igloo form.

Marcelline was a young glaciologist, but also an activist. A militant anti-globalization activist, she was responsible for an Internet site that had contributed to the closing of a Starbucks in China's Forbidden City, seven years after its opening. Since then, she had been working to close the McDonalds in the *Carrousel du Louvre*. In many ways she resembled Rosaire, because she was a woman of conviction, while most modern militants are people of opinion. For her, work and the path to follow were secondary to the result. She wanted to achieve her goals. Marcelline wore blue mascara and painted her nails in black polish while on her right arm, where sailors display anchors or mermaids, there bloomed a half-sleeve of Inuit art tattoos, showing a flying polar bear intertwined with a caribou sticking out its tongue. She spent all her free time in the kitchen with me, and she loved listening to Siouxsie and the Banshees. She fit perfectly the following statistic: 55% of North American women would rather win a Nobel Prize than make love for a year with their fa-

15

vourite celebrity.

Marcelline's happiness was not innate. She cultivated it every day. She found happiness in details. That night, in the cafeteria, she got up from the table to clear off our plates, including hers, untouched. Given my mute disarray, Marcelline, perhaps feeling guilty for having been the messenger of my misfortune, dug out the cooking port hidden in the root cellar under the 10 kilo sack of onions, and poured me a generous serving in a glass full of snow. Even sitting at a beige melamine table, she was as beautiful as ever. She wore very pale jeans, a blue that was almost white, and a sweater too big for her, with snowflake motifs.

"Take a drink, it will calm you."

The six-litre jugs of Australian port were the only alcohol we were able to slip under the radar of the security guards, on the pretext that I needed it for deglazing the roast beef gravy.

"It's cooking wine but it's not too bad, it smells like goldfish, candy, and fizzy nail polish," she said, to draw a smile out of me.

I loved Marcelline, but I had never had the courage to tell her so. She intimidated me. She was too good for me. She was interested in life. With her, every day I learned new things. She had a hundred words to describe the various crystals you can find in ice. She saw patterns of flowers and ferns in the windshields of dump trucks and on frozen lakes.

Marcelline had been hired by Brice de Saxe Majolique, the owner of the mine, to demonstrate that he had an environmental conscience. She had written a doctoral thesis that contained information unpopular with the part-time protestors who preferred Molotov cocktails and broken windows to scientific data. She didn't like phony intellectuals, who were always against everything, and she loved the Inuit, whom she described as a courageous people rich in subtleties. She believed in the power of will and her research had shown that global warming had begun around 1820, at the end of the "Little Ice Age," long before manmade greenhouse gases.

After Marcelline told me about Rosaire's death, I felt I couldn't leave the mine and go to Iqaluit. I decided to keep on working. Marcelline made me understand that it would be easier to not go crazy if I made myself useful. Without her, I might have hunkered down in my tent, immobile on my bed, until someone sent for a medical helicopter to free me from my prostration.

The next day saw the worst morning of my life. I had a terrible head-ache and Kujjuk, my dishwasher, was away; he'd gone to see his sick great-aunt in his native village. In his free time, Kujjuk made jewellery. At my request he had carved from a narwhal tusk a little ring for Marcelline that I had unfortunately broken that winter. He made me another, even more beautiful, that I kept safe in my wallet, waiting for the courage and the best opportunity to offer it to Marcelline. Kujjuk was an unattached male who ingested at least twelve fuzzy peaches per week. An indul-gence that cost his family, which owned the only grocery chain on Baffin Island, $2240 per month. Kujjuk wore aviator glasses that he pushed up on his nose with his index finger fifty times a day. He often cut himself shaving, and stuck little pieces of toilet paper on his skin with calamine lotion to soothe the burning. He was a man of few words. He had lost an arm in a serious meat cutting accident at the age of fourteen. Outside of work, he refused to wear his prosthesis, which he called his "bion-ic hand" in front of children, who looked at him wide-eyed. He never asked a table mate to help him cut his steak: he planted his stump in the middle of the hunk of meat to hold it down, and cut it with a well-honed Swiss Army knife that he always kept in his pocket. Everyone adored Kujjuk, because he knew how to live in the present. Evenings, he slipped THC into the girls' spruce beer martinis and took them home, driving his snowmobile drunk and one-handed on twisty trails in the dark. Once he was almost skewered by a conifer.

Kujjuk was replaced by his cousin, who told me that the mine owner had passed by, and that he wanted to see me that day. Suddenly I was afraid of being fired. The jug of port was still on the cafeteria table, and I had no memory of the night before. Alcohol was not tolerated in the camp under any circumstances. Marcelline came into the kitchen whis-tling with her head buried in her white wolf fur-lined hood, wearing Sorel boots and a blue wool parka, with two Eskimos in a sea kayak em-broidered on the pockets. I smelled the sulphurous odour of the earth's entrails. She'd arrived from her little greenhouse where she grew heir-loom vegetables, including three different kinds of tomatoes no bigger than marbles, under fluorescent bulbs. She dropped her blue string bag onto the kitchen's steel counter. Inside were the tomatoes: tiny *Tetons de*

Venus, little Black Krims and a dozen *Andine Cornues*. Marcelline was a bringer of miracles. I cut the tomatoes into tiny slices, scented them with a single leaf of Labrador tea and some shredded sorrel from the tundra, and then devoured them as though they were her heart. She was oblivious. She didn't know that on summer nights, when the midnight sun made sleep impossible, I sat on the rocky eye crawling with tender green lichen, just outside the camp that looked down on Hudson's Bay and beyond to Ungava Bay, and wrote to her. She thought that like her, I was listening to the cracking of the ice, ten million year-old sounds, but I was writing to her in a spiral notebook. *Every day I am afraid of you*. Missives that I tore up once the sun had set.

"This morning I went down into the mine to see our Eldorado. I like studying veins of gold. It seems to me they send out vibrations that heal our bad moods. You should go and see what twists and turns in the earth's crust, Ambroise."

"You shouldn't go down in the mine, it's too dangerous. Your work is to observe how ice retreats. Mine is to prepare fish fillets."

"Sometimes I get tired of playing the surveyor, of measuring rocky nodules. I need to put myself in danger. It's not up to you to tell me what to do."

"You aren't afraid of gas? Last week a hundred and seven Chinese miners were found dead after an explosion."

"Listen, Ambroise, in the nineteenth century miners took a canary down in the mine and if the bird got restless, they came right back up. Today it's much less dangerous."

"I once had a girlfriend who swallowed so much gin and tonic that she drank water out of toilet bowls in bars. Let's just say that you, Marcelline, you put yourself in danger in a more complicated way. Will I be able to save you from your death wish?"

"It's not up to you to save me."

"Here, no one gets off scot-free. All the white managers are looking for a great grandmother with one-eighth native blood in order to get Indian status and not pay taxes or electric bills, and to be able to to hunt out of season. It's assisted death."

Marcelline was no longer listening to me. She went over to Tommy, the pilot, sitting in the cafeteria.

So there I was, with the dark and weird idea that Marcelline's life was in peril and that I ought to protect her, as if her entire existence was hanging by a thread. When I worried about her, she threw me scathing looks. Marcelline lost patience. She didn't understand my lack of insight, my inability to read her thoughts and desires. In this land of glaciers, I failed to be in sync with her. My protective instinct, exacerbated by the loss of my brother, got on her nerves.

6

The Gold Panner

Having become a Marxist at eighteen, Brice de Saxe Majolique was the first of his family line in a millennium to do any work. His mother liked to say that his family was one of those that had been policy advisors to the Medicis. She usually followed up this declaration with a laugh like the cry of a wolverine preparing to dismember its prey. In fact, Brice's ancestors had cultivated a melon farm near one of their summer residences, garnering him his first nickname - the Melon Prince. Weary of monitoring the shifting shades of yellow as the day ran on, from the vantage point of the sofa covered in faded embroidery that had held pride of place in the family salon since the seventeenth century, Brice de Saxe Majolique decided to go to work, despite the hysterical laughter the decision elicited from his cousins, who still aspired to the idle life afforded by the Mediterranean Riviera.

Brice de Saxe Majolique was not a prophet, but he was a prince, and that charmed the ladies. He had a poetic vision of work. An eccentric prince-cum-prospector, Brice de Saxe Majolique had taken his time choosing a vocation. His experiences as an entrepreneur were varied. He was a taxidermist in Paris for ten years, but it was in the Canadian Arctic Archipelago that he became a panner for gold: someone seeking deposits in stream beds. That won him the nickname, the Gold Panning Prince. Full of enthusiasm, he bought parcels of land for a pittance and set up a gold mine at Kimmirut, to which he gave the pretty name,

Chrysostom Inc. The day the mine opened he had a gold crown fitted over his left front tooth, for good luck.

That morning, after offering me the tomatoes, Marcelline had breakfast with Tommy the pilot and left for work without saying good bye. I didn't have time to tell her that I'd been summoned by the big boss, who might be about to fire me for having imbibed alcohol the night before. I left the kitchen briefly to catch my breath and to inhale the metallic odour emanating from the mine. Even on calm days, in Kimmirut the air was saturated with the smell of carats from below ground: talc, gypsum, gold. The thin layer of snow seemed to have been crocheted by a lacemaker on the black cliffs of volcanic rock, while a tern touched down right in front of me. I made a wish, thinking of the day my father stapled a sparrow's wing into Rosaire's palm, proclaiming that if he wanted to be free he had to learn to fly. I was wearing my green cap, the one with the LG-3 hydroelectric station logo, and a red hunting shirt. The cold air began to freeze the liquid in my eyeballs, but I didn't want to go back in. In this part of the world you don't stay outside very long, even in spring, for fear that your lungs will turn into tanks of ice. Rosaire again. Even as an adult, his presence always affected me like the cow's breath warming the infant in the manger. I was just starting to absorb his absence when overhead, a snowy owl let out a cry that made me jump. In his claws, tight to his body, he was holding a little fish so it wouldn't freeze. It was the first time I had seen this bird hunting in the middle of the day. It seemed strange. Just then, I heard from far off the mine owner's voice.

Brice de Saxe Majolique always made himself heard long before you could see him. He behaved like the viceroy of Baffin Island. Behind me, I heard him shouting into his cell phone: "Anyway, I only sleep three nights a week. I'm too busy. I can't afford to sleep. Sleep smells of death. You'll have to talk to my secretary if you want an appointment. I'm a mining prospector and my company's listed on the stock exchange."

Marie-Perle, the star stripper he brought to the mine every other weekend, was dogging his footsteps. They came towards me in their white Canada Goose coats. The girl's hood was covered in Arctic fox fur, his in Arctic hare. Brice pocketed his phone and embraced Marie-Perle in the midst of yellow trucks nine storeys high. In their coats puffed up with goose feathers, they couldn't hold their arms down along their sides, and they looked like a couple of Care Bears come to offer me their pointless sympathies. Rumour had it, according to the drillers, that the boss and his dancer-secretary had once been caught in a compromising position around midnight on Level 3 of the mine, their headlamps bobbing to the rhythm of their lovemaking.

Marie-Perle came up to talk to me first. Her eyes were a galvanized blue. She opened her mouth and out came this indignity:

"Ambroise, I'm really sorry about your brother. He was handsome and smart. All the women in Iqaluit dreamed of marrying him. But he just wanted to hang around with that slut, Lumi. She got it wrong. As far as I'm concerned, you're the better of the two. Your faces are alike, but not the rest. Why are you so shy? The girls think you aren't interested..."

I am very tall. That's about all I have in common with my brother, physically. My beard is full and black, his was blond and nearly non-existent. When he stopped shaving during hockey tournaments, his beard grew out in patches and looked like the curly hair of Russian princesses. I could well imagine what Marie-Perle might think of it. Brice de Saxe Majolique wore ski goggles in which I could only see my own image upside down. Suddenly the gold panner spoke, without removing his mirrored lenses:

"In this land of ice, anything can happen. Your brother made a great contribution to the cause of the Inuit. His life served us all."

I slung my hunting rifle over my shoulder and climbed onto the snowmobile parked near three fat frozen fish stuck upright in the snow. I wanted to end this conversation as fast as I could.

"Thanks to you both," I replied, before putting the vehicle in gear and taking off over ice so thin that it was blue.

If I'd been like my brother, I would have capitalized on this encounter with the boss to ask for a raise or a promotion. That morning, I simply fled towards the mine's exit. I've always had trouble asserting myself. I hated this Brice de Saxe Majolique. When he lingered in the kitchen, his greyhound grabbed sugar cubes from the serving table with its tongue. Its master pretended not to see.

7

The New Klondike

The word *glace* was used for the first time in the West by Chrétien de Troyes to describe a mirror. In the land of precious metals, I had the impression of being a replica of myself, of seeing my image reflected everywhere: in frozen water when we were flying over Viscount Melville Sound; in the pink mountains at sunset; in the aurora borealis that undulated like teal silk curtains in the black sky. In Nunavut nature gave no one preferential treatment: all men were fragile and had no choice but to tell the truth or risk losing their lives.

The gold mine was located behind what the Inuit called the Violet Rock, towards the north, two days by dogsled from Iqaluit, the capital of Nunavut. The inhabitants of Baffin Island loved to say that that all the elements of the Periodic Table were abundantly present in their subsoil. Here at one time pots had been exchanged for sealskin mittens. Now twin-engine planes full of tourists tracked icebergs almost the size of France and unlucky whalers were drawn into the deeps with their crews by cetaceans weighing tons. On Baffin Island, Whites came to work with the idea of making their fortunes thanks to inflated salaries and the thought of putting an enormous nugget of raw gold in the pockets of their jackets. A nugget that would pay for their children's and grandchildren's university education and their retirement as well.

Brice de Saxe Majolique was the sort of man who refused to admit guilt. He could deny anything, even stealing from a church when its steeple was protruding from his coat. Disowning those Marxist ideas that had led him to take up work, he had developed a competitive zeal that defied understanding. In the North, it's easy to make a fortune. The possibilities are many. At the mine, the salary scale began with Kujjuk, my dishwasher, future inheritor of the supermarket chain Nordis-Coop, who earned seventy dollars an hour. We worked twelve hours per day, seven days a week, for four weeks. The Kimmurut mine was dry; drugs and alcohol were prohibited. Every three months we had the right to two weeks' vacation, which most people spent in the South.

I rode my snowmobile to the shell hole. That's where I went at low tide to gather scallops. The place was wrapped in silence. I stopped the vehicle. Still thinking about Rosaire, I was overcome by sadness. I also thought about my own life before Marcelline arrived at the camp: the routine, the fish fillets, the wan hue of the fluorescent tubes. Marcelline was a source of constant anxiety for me. Her strange gold-bearing scent obsessed me. I knew, however, that she only loved things that were unable to love her back. The mathematical equations with which she covered pages of her spiral notebook, for instance. Or the ancient strawberry plants that she tried in vain to grow in her improbable greenhouse. I was afraid of being fired because of the jug of port forgotten on the table and being left with absolutely nothing. I put a few sea scallops in my pocket. The ice was cracking under the weight of my snowmobile. I went back to camp.

In the cafeteria, the pilots were talking about my brother. The conversation stopped abruptly when I approached their table. Arctic pilots often give tourists their first culture shock. Dressed in denim overalls, with a heavy coat, a fur tuque and work boots, they sometimes played at being flight attendants, offering sandwiches wrapped in cellophane to the passengers. But what was most disconcerting was when they left the controls of the plane to go and rummage in the cargo hold. The little Russian planes that served the tiny villages of the Arctic Archipelago dated from the Second World War. I was afraid for Marcelline, who traveled frequently on those machines, because they often ended up at the bottoms of lakes. I was also afraid for Tommy, the Inuit pilot, with whom I shared a tent in the camp. He worked for one of the biggest airline companies in Nunavut. The airplanes of Sundog Air looked like delivery trucks with wings. Affectionately described by the pilots as flying Winnebagos, the Skyvan SC-17s had cargo holds as big as a whale.

Seated over his third coffee and an apple turnover, Tommy was telling a group of pilots the rumour of the week, whose source was the mechanics: Brice de Saxe Majolique suffered from cyanopsia, a disorder of the retina that made everything look blue.

"It's a side effect of Viagra," remarked one of the pilots.

"Brice often asks me to bring him pharmaceutical products from Mexico, but never Viagra," returned Tommy.

"Ho ho, look who's trying to protect Brice! He must get it through the Internet," put in the youngest pilot, before getting a tap upside his head.

Tommy was born in an igloo. He always seemed to be hiding something under his coat and his square face was made for the camera. The previous week I'd seen Marcelline jump for joy and applaud when the pilot showed her the enormous gloves of baby seal that his grandfather had left him. He wore a necklace of caribou teeth strung on a leather thong and used traditional snowshoes, also with leather thongs, which he had strung himself. He hated the more modern snowshoes, in titanium, that you ordered from a catalogue. Every other week he rolled back the collar of his brushed cotton shirt to see what island of the Polar Archipelago the hickey on his neck resembled. That day it was Ellesmere, where he was born. In the Arctic, the key question was to know who had gone farthest north. If Tommy was part of the game, and he often initiated it, he won hands down. He was born at Grise Fiord, "there where the snow never melts" in Inuktitut. A hamlet of a hundred and forty inhabitants, the farthest north in Canada. His family, which long ago had lived in Inukjuak, in the fertile tundra, had like so many others been displaced by the government to populate the Arctic desert and to reinforce Canada's presence in the North. Its members had been promised houses, but they only got tents. They'd been guaranteed an abundance of game, but they found themselves with no means of support. They'd been assured that it would be possible to return to Inukjuak if they didn't like the place, but they had been left to survive on their own. This story made my nose bleed whenever I thought of it.

Tommy always had a Bud Light cooler in his plane. It contained ice from his home bay to make tea with. According to him, the expanse of uneven ice, resembling skin with goose bumps, was less polluted north of the seventieth parallel. Marcelline always tried to refute him. He listened to Dolly Parton, the volume cranked up, in his twin engine, and he dried seal or caribou skins on the outside of our tent. In his bed he warmed up his girls with a Polartec blanket, which depicted a wolf bearing its teeth .One day Marcelline asked me if I had noticed that Tommy's hands had the texture of driftwood. What I had noticed was that he often wore a Property of Mexico sweater and that the password for his alarm system was Playa del Carmen. For him, mescal was a woman's drink. He preferred, by far, tequila with a scorpion in the bottom of the bottle. He also wore cowboy boots made of boa constrictor skin, with the stuffed head at the very tip. In the North, people are always larger than life.

Marcelline seemed to have disappeared, and I was worried. I opened my shells over the sink and ate two scallops raw. The next day Tommy would drive me to Iqaluit so that the death of my brother would at last be real to me. I'd be asked to sign the official papers, and I'd see his remains. I would have preferred to believe that it was all just a rumour, that nothing had really happened, and that I could feel the warmth of Rosaire's body again as he embraced me at the airport.

8

Drinkable Gold

There were no more cigarettes in the entire Kimmirut camp, so Kujjuk's cousin rolled pages of *Newsweek* into makeshift substitutes. The solvent in the inks sometimes induced dark deliriums. Fashion magazines, though rare here, were even more effective. An issue of *Vogue* stolen from Marie-Perle had lasted a whole year. My replacement dishwasher suddenly said to me:

"I saw my cousin carving a ring for you from narwhal ivory. He said it was for your future fiancée. Did she find it beautiful?"

"I'm waiting for the best time to give it to her. Right now is not ideal."

That night fatigue muddled my words. After the evening meal service I remained alone on the shore and watched the sun set. I spotted a Novaya Zemlya effect, or a rectangular sun, caused by the light's refraction near the pole. And then I thought of Rosaire: he often said that I was lucky to live like the Inuit and to possess nothing. Indeed, I owned neither an egg beater, nor furniture, nor a house. A woman even less. Rosaire told me that Brice de Saxe Majolique's problem was his property rights, his prospecting permit, his mineral strategies, his businesses that ate up his time. All of it needed protecting. It made him vulnerable.

The Kimmirut mine was surrounded by a double electric fence and guarded by two Inuit armed with rifles who thought they were protecting polar bears from the white man, a real danger for the species. They didn't know that the bears they sometimes captured never again saw the ice field. Those bears were the delight of every zoo in the European Community, where their fur often became greyish green, sullied by blue algae and poor hygienic conditions. Brice de Saxe Majolique's behaviour was akin to that of the first explorers who, ever since the tenth century, had offered European kings live polar bears as diplomatic gifts. The land, the men, the fauna and flora - all of it belonged to Brice de Saxe Majolique.

Marcelline got carried away easily. I loved to see her get angry with me. It was the only way I could make this beauty think of me – she who smelled of bubble bath in a place where the odour of jerrycans predominated. That night I threw in the oven a hundred and forty-four dozen frozen apple turnovers, the only foodstuff really favoured by the technicians. Now and then I tried to treat them to something else. I even brewed the thorns of small blackberry bushes to make highly scented traditional teas, I prepared trifles with arctic blueberries, tarts with young shoots of white spruce, omelettes with boletuses and arctic willow. Nothing doing. Most of the men only gorged themselves on those vile factory-made apple turnovers and slices of overcooked roast beef. My work was less heroic than Tommy's, even if it had more popular appeal, and to make myself more interesting in Marcelline's eyes, I talked to her about Rosaire:

"Last year, my brother discovered in the woods behind my parents' house an ancient wooden pietà nailed to a tree. It must have belonged to our ancestor Jean Nicolet, who presented it to the French missionary brothers after his attempt to discover the route to China. It had survived the burning of a church in 1916 and the grasshopper attacks in 1932, when the village where it ended up was abandoned. My uncle found the statue years later, and hid it in an elm behind our house." I quickly concluded: "It remained well hidden in the tree, because the bark had gradually closed over the statue."

"My only family heirloom comes from my grandmother. A dozen rose petals that I gathered from the enormous wreath that adorned her coffin."

She took from her jeans pocket a small plastic bag containing the petals, dried and in fragments. With Rosaire's disappearance, I knew that it would be awkward now to confess my love for Marcelline. I kept it to myself. Two days earlier I had told myself that if Marcelline accepted my marriage proposal, I would take her on a trip to a deserted polar island. In the white dunes of the arctic desert, we would open an environmental hotel with the name *Sinnak,* which means *to sleep* in Inuktitut. Ten little cabins on the ice for fishing. We would offer gold therapy treatments, according to the ancient practices of Helvétius, who made from rosemary oil drinkable gold to cure melancholy. The cabins' roofs would be supported by caribou jaws. The bed linen would be the colour of bleached bones. People would sleep on chairs made from recycled antlers woven together by a retired Norwegian architect. I would cook all day and I'd serve aquavit made from lichen; bannock, a thick, round, compact bread, with sea parsley; and elixirs of gold. The windows would look out on the ice field, framed by sea glass curtains of indigo, pink, and canary yellow. We would never wash and our skin would become as dark as leather. With Marcelline, life would no longer be a punishment.

9

The Art of the Scintillator

Marcelline was sitting at the counter reading the *Baffin Daily News*. I'd have liked to be brave enough to lie down on the slab of cold granite and kiss her. But my self-esteem was too low for me to dare take such an initiative. My dishwasher whipped up a traditional fish head soup so smelly that it "can make birds drop from the sky," he assured me. Marcelline started reading the paper aloud to distract me

"Listen to this: after downing some frozen apples found in a container behind the Co-op, a drunk caribou gored the former vicar of the Saint Jude church in Iqaluit. I can't believe it!"

"The apples must have fermented and turned into alcohol. Animals love alcohol. When we were younger, Rosaire and I once fed six beers to a black bear. Then he devoured a platter of twenty pre-wrapped egg sandwiches."

"The bear had the munchies," she giggled.

"Then he opened a can of pears with one slap of his paw and glugged it down."

Marcelline had again buried herself in her paper:

"A dispatch from AFP says there was a spectacular robbery at the Louvre: the throne of Christian V, made of narwhal tusks, was spirited away on the night of May third."

"Narwhal tusks were for a long time advertised and sold as unicorn horns, because the narwhal is a shy animal, and therefore rare. The horns sometimes changed hands for more than ten times their weight in gold," I went on, to impress her.

"You know, according to an old superstition I heard somewhere or other, every big theft from the Louvre is followed by a world war. *The Mona Lisa* was taken in 1911, and Watteau's *l'Indifférent* in 1939," remarked Marcelline.

A war whose stakes were global was perhaps brewing behind our backs in the Arctic Archipelago. Russian and Chinese drones were flying over and mapping the territory. Ships flying Russian flags were being chased off international waters by the Canadian coast guard.

I thought I'd be able to take off for Iqaluit that morning, but a sudden shower, along with a snow squall, bore down on the camp, delaying my departure. I had to wait. Patience is an indispensable weapon on Baffin Island. No trip is simple. Meteorological conditions, not men, run the country.

I couldn't help thinking that the circumstances surrounding Rosaire's death had greater implications than I'd suspected. Rosaire had recently worked on a number of cases, one of which had led the government to apologize to Inuit families like Tommy's that had been transferred to the High Arctic. The Arctic was a possible focal point for armed conflict. The Inuit, more than ever, were essential allies.

A month before Rosaire's death, Brice de Saxe Majolique called a staff meeting. From his elevated podium, with his lambskin aviator cap turned back to front, he preached like a Baptist pastor, fist lifted to the sky. Marie-Perle, his future fiancée, in a green silk dress stippled with gold stars, sat in the front row, knees together, chin raised, back erect. She looked at him with a student's adoration. He loved to motivate his troops by telling them that Canada was determined to defend its interests in the Arctic. He declaimed, bringing his fist down on the lectern, that our country was the world's richest in natural resources, which were right there under the ice beneath our feet. He spluttered that the European nations would soon be dependent on others and would have to conquer colonies in order to survive, whereas Canada would remain self-sufficient with its reserves of water, diamonds, gold, natural gas, oil, uranium and precious stones of all sorts. I already saw Marie-Perle adorned with a lapis-lazuli diadem and holding a sceptre encrusted with tourmaline, finally crowned queen, a ridiculous gold-pan Queen.

On Baffin Island you saw scientists everywhere, scintillators in hand, paving the way for the new Klondike. Prospecting permits and plots of land were being sold by the government to citizens all over the Arctic Archipelago for three thousand dollars to reassert its sovereignty in the region.

Brice de Saxe Majolique, as a good prospector, holding a stone with veins of gold running through it, explained to his employees, all sporting helmets with the mine's logo, that Canadians would soon be very rich. Everyone seemed to want his slice of the pie. I stood at the back with Rosaire, arms crossed, taking in the delirious assembly. Our so-called gold panner was like Saint John Chrysostom, the archbishop, known as "golden mouthed": he employed the rhetorical tricks of gurus. My brother said to me that day:

"Myself, I would pour liquid gold down the throats of all those liars to shut them up. The Chinese already claim part of our territory, talking about 'international waters' to absolve themselves."

At the start of the twenty-first century, the melting of the ice was making for an increasingly extensive exploration of the Arctic. And Brice de Saxe Majolique wanted to write the book on this new adventure. September 2, 2008, had been an important historical landmark: a former oil tanker, transformed into a cruise ship, had crossed through the Northwest Passage, where Franklin had once run aground. Brice de Saxe Majolique, with his gold tooth, was aboard that ship as it brought to light a new Panama Canal. This passage would enable Europeans to connect with Asia, while shortening their voyage by seven thousand kilometres and two weeks of navigation. Millions of dollars were at stake. Virgin land hidden by ice and still unknown to man would be discovered and at last mapped out. Brice de Saxe Majolique said that he had felt at that historic moment the same emotion as Magellan circling the globe. "My name is now part of history," he had murmured to journalists waiting for the crew on the dock.

The exploitation of the subsoil was a question that excited the passions of all Canadians, and the new army base near Kimmirut was evidence of this. Lumi, the stripper who had found my brother's lifeless body, liked to hang out with the young soldiers who passed through Iqaluit. She said they were so young that some still missed their mothers. She would ask each one she picked up, "What's the most precious thing you own?"

This question served to console them. Though they were far from home, they lacked for nothing. Not with Lumi, in any case. Unbeknownst to my brother, she spent time with Gauthier Mercure, a twenty-two year old infantry sergeant, who had joined the Canadian army to study engineering. He loved submarines and appreciated the gravitas a uniform confers on a young man. He even wore it evenings in the Arctic Circle bar.

Although their relationship had been short-lived, Rosaire had been mesmerized by the beautiful Lumi: he had written our mother to announce that he was going to marry a young Inuit with black hair. He had offered Lumi a cabochon with eight sapphires from a mine near Kimmirut. She had not said no to his marriage proposal, but she hadn't said yes either. She had calmly explained that she would prefer him to take out an insurance policy in her name than to have her wear this enormous jewel.

Lumi was very interested in soldiers, because she knew that they were privy to state secrets, that they were aware of things that common mortals did not know. Often, in the evening, when the sergeant was confined to his barracks, they talked on MSN, and it was then, strangely, that he gave her the most information, doubtless to keep her attention. And so he had sent her a document that would change everything. The Canadian government wanted to regain control of Nunavut to protect its interests in the Arctic, with an official agreement declaring that native people had no rights to the subsoil and mineral exploitation. Lumi was disgusted. Even France, out of Saint Pierre and Miquelon, was trying to obtain rights to the seabed bordering on Labrador. The land of ice was a veritable powder keg in the making.

10

Galileo's Finger

On May 5th, after a long early morning when the squall gave way to endless drifting snow, I was able to take time off for the return trip to Iqaluit to see my brother's remains. Before leaving, Tommy the pilot ate an apple turnover in the cafeteria with Marcelline at his side. I served Inuit children raw trout and thought about my parents. About how my mother was going to be destroyed by this terrible news. All at once my grief would become contagious.

The airplane was very noisy on takeoff, and we flew over a colony of arctic terns at low altitude, where the females had eaten their little ones. Tommy shouted to make his voice heard over the noise of the engines:

"Since the beginning of the year there've been supernatural fish harvests all over the planet. Giant squid have turned up near the Golden Gate Bridge in San Francisco. A 450 kilo tuna was caught off Osaka. A fisherman in Greenland netted a two-horned narwhal. Near Iqaluit, a polar bear died after swallowing a scintillator left on the ground by a bureaucrat from Environment Canada, and the schools of arctic char are so huge that you can fish them by hand."

From the plane, the enormous expanse of ice was like a Rorschach test, and I took stock of the huge stakes it represented for our country. The Inuit considered the ice as part of their territory, because they moved around on it as on dry land to hunt and fish. They walked on water. But the white man, master of laws and treaties foreign to such ancient traditions, saw this icy surface as "international waters."

Reading the *Baffin Daily News* to distract myself, I saw that Mitsy Cooper, a Radio-Canada journalist responsible for circumpolar affairs, was making hay with the mysterious circumstances surrounding the death of the lawyer Rosaire Nicolet. Mitsy was one of those women whose complexion betrayed a British paleness, a blonde with black roots and lips bitten till they bled, who roamed the bars of Iqaluit every night smoking long menthol cigarettes and wearing motorcycle gloves perforated at the knuckles. She smoked like a Greek, even when skiing downhill at Grey Rocks. She had begun to comb through Rosaire's life, and to recount offbeat stories about him in the papers. My brother liked women and p*ink fixes*, a mixture of cocaine and chilli powder, made popular by Tommy after one of his trips to Mexico. He put a few drops of Tabasco sauce in his coffee, because hot peppers stimulated the production of adrenaline and contained natural opiates. The article then quoted Marie-Perle, who was more than happy to reveal that Rosaire had met Lumi in a brothel. I put the paper down at my feet, repelled by such intimate information suddenly brought to light.

Rosaire often talked about his first weekends with Lumi, when they'd hunted twenty-four wild geese and plucked them in his garage. When they opened the mechanical door, a cloud of white down had taken off towards the Perseids sky. He was the happiest of men to be embracing a woman as free as Lumi. The next day a fussy neighbour found four feathers on his well-groomed lawn and tossed them angrily into Rosaire's yard. Months later Rosaire still had the goose feathers in his house, and they remained a source of laughter and happiness.

According to Mitsy, Lumi had not seemed saddened by Rosaire's death. The young Inuit was known for her acerbity and her spiteful words, and I'd always suspected her of wanting to infect my brother with her slow poison. Exasperated, I picked up the paper again. Rosaire had often borne the brunt of Lumi's anger and coldness. I knew that Rosaire honoured the four-minute rule, which says that the first moments of daily get-togethers, after work for instance, determine the course of an entire evening. "If you argue within that time, you've had it!" he insisted. I couldn't understand how the journalist could have got her hands on such information. All those intimate revelations, pell mell, enraged me.

Mitsy Cooper couldn't be thirty. Under her North Face coat she often wore a silk camisole with thin straps and claimed to be hot even when it was forty below. I always thought she had a crush on Rosaire.

I hate plane travel because turbulence makes me nauseated. I thought about Marcelline. I was anxious to see her again. She was also leaving camp that day, on a medical flight to Grise Fiord, where she was to study a glacial constriction for future prospectors. My visit to Iqaluit would only last a few hours. Its small coloured houses were built without foundations, on frozen soil. When you approached from the air they seemed simply to have been set down on the ground, and with the melting of the permafrost due to climate change, they tilted slightly to the left.

The police authorities asked me if I wanted to send my brother's body south to Montreal after the medical examiner had seen him. For the moment, the cause of death was unknown. I thought of my mother and I said yes, we would bury him in Montreal. I was certain, however, that Rosaire would have rather been buried in the permafrost of an Arctic island, and have the earth draw him down to its core. Like all those who truly live in the present, he had not foreseen his death: there was no will.

I had to identify the body before it was moved. There was no morgue in Iqaluit, and the remains were kept cold in a big airplane hangar near the airport. He was laid out on a stretcher, in a blue bag, like one of those plastic groundsheets used for camping. The officer undid the yellow plastic zipper, and I clearly heard it slide the length of the bag. Seeing my brother's face, I expected him to speak, to say he was happy to see me, that everything was going to be all right, but he was mute and motionless. I couldn't recognize him. But I said to the officer that this was indeed Rosaire Nicolet, my older brother, a lawyer in international law. I took his hand and I kissed him. I got down on my knees at the foot of Rosaire's body and I wept.

I kept his hand in mine for a long time, the hand whose index finger had been amputated. He had lost it in the Arctic, after a kayak expedition that went wrong. All had begun well. The morning of our departure I heard him tell an electrician in the mine cafeteria that he admired me, because I'd just obtained my trapper's diploma after only three weeks of training. My brother admired me? That gave me confidence and calmed my nerves. Tommy had a few days of vacation ahead of him, and suggested going with us in a sea kayak for the weekend, through the long crevasses that split the ocean's ice plates. At the time I felt more secure with him around. The morning light had come down on us like a breath, and it looked to be a miraculous day. I was enthusiastic at the thought of picnicking in the great virgin spaces, and I'd prepared *cordetta* for the road, little mini-brochettes of grilled organs, plus a *petit Jésus,* a dry sausage you ate with a knife and *coppa di testa*, a head cheese studded with blueberries. Rosaire, happy, laughed like a whale. We had seen the tracks left in the snow by a mother bear and her cub. The little one had jumped on its mother's back to be carried for a few kilometres. On the second day of our expedition though, an unexpected blizzard had come up. Tommy's kayak, with our supplies, was split by jagged ice and over-turned. All the cargo was lost at once, and we were left with no resources. We had to walk for forty-six hours to find the Kimmirut camp, in a temperature close to forty below Celsius. Since then, expeditions of that sort have been forbidden to employees. Rosaire lost a little bit of his index finger in this misadventure. He had to have it amputated just below the first joint, because serious frostbite threatened the rest of his hand.

The mine nurse was not on duty, she wouldn't arrive until two days later. The North is a strange place: things happen there that are unthinkable elsewhere. It was none other than Brice de Saxe Majolique himself who amputated Rosaire's finger. He claimed to have done his military service in Sudan and to have worked in an infirmary where he'd learned how to cauterize wounds inflicted by machetes. But Brice de Saxe Majolique had also said he'd met two hundred year old men in China... During the operation he sat on a fluorescent pink Danon milk crate in front of the shower tent. I don't remember ever having witnessed something so surreal and painful.

The novice doctor cauterized the wound and covered the stump with whale blubber and mud, then tied a tourniquet of fine leather cord around Rosaire's wrist. My brother, miraculously, survived. An eternal optimist, who loved turning everything into an activity or a competition, he even mummified the tip of his index finger according to ancient techniques he had learned from *National Geographic*. To mark the event and celebrate his survival, it had to be cleaned, embalmed, and placed in a wooden box filled with Labrador tea and mountain sorrel. The box was then set out to dry in the desert of ice under the Rock of Violets for forty days. I often wondered if the amputation had really been necessary, or if it was Brice's revenge in disguise. The Inuit say: "If you cannot cut off your enemy's head, you must kiss it."

Rosaire's mummified index finger was dear to him, and he kept it in a little finger-shaped gold reliquary. It was proof that he had cheated death. That day, he had counted out the number of springs he had still to live and declared: "Fifty." With the passing of time, he spoke often of that index finger and showed the "mummy" to girls to get a rise out of them. When he did so, too often for my tastes, he made the connection between his index finger and that of Galileo, a finger of the greatest importance to polar explorers. Galileo had been condemned for teaching that the earth moved around the sun, and not the opposite. His index finger, with which he had often pointed to the stars and the nebulae, was mummified, deposited in a common glass jar filled with formaldehyde, and placed in a museum in Florence. Rosaire had the gift of projecting himself into the lives of famous men, while I was content to cook for those nobody knew.

An officer gave me a plastic bag that held my brother's belongings, and I was astonished to find inside it the old yellow notebook containing the information our uncle had set down concerning our ancestor Jean Nicolet. Why had Rosaire brought it with him to Iqaluit?

11

A Chinese Man before Columbus

While waiting for the plane back I looked through the notebook I had found among my brother's things. It was filled with hand-written letters and clippings from penny papers. I turned the pages slowly, because many of them showed traces of mould. I read that in May, 1614, maritime navigation was very fashionable. In France, women wore hair-dos resembling a sailboat's stern. In the Luxembourg Gardens at night, men with eyes glued to the ends of their telescopes, scrutinized the stars. Everywhere people were talking about a possible sea route to the West, with as much hope as those who dreamed of transforming lead into gold. A statue of the Virgin was drawn freehand on the inside of the cover. My brother had begun to write the story of our ancestor in the yellow note-book. I recognized his penmanship, as ornate as that of a woman.

Before setting out for the New World, Jean Nicolet, who was not yet thirteen years old, had been drawn to a leaflet distributed by the vocations service of the Diocese of Paris. He had found the card on the square outside the chapel dedicated to Saint Suzanne.

What calling for your life? Priesthood, marriage, or a life of devotion? How to know to where God is calling you? A retreat of discernment. A service for feminine vocations. See Father Hyacinthe de L'Épervier, ordination of deacons.

Jean Nicolet, simple son of a postal messenger for the king and Marguerite de la Mer, did not want to follow in his father's footsteps. He wanted to enter holy orders in order to study. He loved geography and had dreamed throughout his childhood of becoming a missionary in China. His brother was a priest, and thanks to his perseverance, Nicolet was named assistant archivist with the Sulpician sisters. He classified thousands of documents, holy pictures, and illuminated manuscripts. He felt that he was living at the heart of a story that seemed to have been lost in boxes, chests and files. To be surrounded by all these objects from the past made him happy. One day he found a mappemonde of Chinese origin, preserved between two sheets of violet tissue paper and dated 1418, which described the location and the contours of America. Having discovered this map, which had lain dormant in the Sulpician archives for nearly two centuries, Nicolet exclaimed to himself:

"A Chinese man before Columbus?"

The map bore the seal of the famous Chinese admiral Zheng He, a eunuch who had circumnavigated the world long before Magellan. Nicolet kept his discovery secret, because he knew that such information would not be well received. He did not want the deacon to destroy this mappemonde, inscribed on fine paper derived from mulberry bark and glued onto a piece of linen.

He was afraid that the deacon would claim that he himself had found it. Actually, Jean Nicolet had had thoughts of stealing it. He'd begun to draw reproductions on copy paper, then on butcher's paper, before he made a final version, his hand having become surer, on a large sheet of Arches paper. What Nicolet did not know was that the map in question had been stolen from Chinese diplomats by Christopher Columbus's right hand men, that it had been referred to during the three voyages and that it had subsequently been forgotten in the religious archives.

Christopher Columbus was known for his wide knowledge, especially in the field of astronomy. In Jamaica, aware that an eclipse of the sun was imminent, he had rebuked the rebellious villagers and threatened to make the sun disappear for some minutes in order to punish them. As a result he was viewed as a divinity and he won the Jamaicans over without having to use force. To master the movement of the stars was to command the language of the gods.

Some days after the discovery of this map, Nicolet, now sober and pensive, had a crucial encounter. In the Écorcherie tavern in the middle of Paris, seven of the richest merchants in Europe were sitting around a table and drinking gin. An admiral among them, who had already over-imbibed, trumpeted that he would soon be setting out to sea, bound for an unknown land, "to face the sea monsters," as he repeated time and again.

That night, in inviting himself to the admiral's table, Nicolet altered the course of his destiny. Together they drank to women's charms and sang to brotherhood and reason. Above all, they talked about the North Star and frozen seas. Nicolet, who could not return drunk to the archives, and so had no place to sleep, helped his new friend the admiral to find his way home. Young Nicolet, also drunk, fell asleep on the living room floor.

It was one of those unforeseeable moments when life takes a turn that gives you a miraculous second chance. In the uneasy sleep of his first night of drunkenness, Jean dreamed of his Chinese map. In the early morning, as the bells of Saint-Sulpice church rang out softly, beckoning the sisters of the congregation to their first prayer, he left the admiral's dwelling with, under his coat, a poker that he'd found near the fireplace. It was five o'clock. Night was slowly lifting its velvet cloak from the city. The moon, in a white halo, augured better days.

Nicolet, still tipsy, made his way to the archives office, forced the door, and stole the Chinese mappemonde, thinking it would be easy to sell to curious sailors or serious navigators. This map seemed to point a way to China sailing west. A route towards riches, an abundance of cinnamon bark, slender pods of vanilla and intoxicating nutmeg, deadly if over-consumed..

The sun lent an orange hue to the fronts of buildings. The girls of Paris slept in the shelter of alcoves or behind bushes in the big park facing the archives building. He noticed that one of them had a cleft lip and wore a flesh-coloured dress covered with soot. She was snoring. Paris seemed frozen in silence. Jean Nicolet chose to take his life in his hands.

Three blows from the poker to the copper lock embellished with two winged goats were enough to make it give way. No one saw Jean Nicolet enter the building. He was certain that the archivists, inundated with documents, did not know about this map. The sisters of the congregation would have no notion of its disappearance, because for them it had been "lost" in the archives for a long time. Jean had cautiously placed it in a wooden filing cabinet along with accounting books from 1492. It was in the fifth drawer, the one with a handle in the shape of a small porcelain dove. He carefully rolled the map into a piece of damask stolen from the textile archive and left over from a costume made for Louis X to wear at his coronation in 1314. He chose to leave by the grand staircase, where he was surprised by a young novice hoping to display her devotion and courage by starting work at the crack of dawn.

"Jean Nicolet, what are you doing here?"

"I just wanted to get the bundle of letters my late mother wrote to me. I couldn't sleep," answered Nicolet.

There was sweat on his brow. The novice grabbed Jean by the wrist and tried to relieve him of the damask roll.

"You got up at dawn to steal from the community that has offered you so much? This cloth has historic value!" exclaimed the indignant novice.

Polynya

Nicolet punched the novice in the nose, and she fell down the stairs. Getting up, she chased the fugitive to the other side of the bridge, crying:

"God will learn about your sin!"

Nicolet was already far away. He ran as fast as he could, the map in his hand.

12

I Will Always Love You

The wait was long, but I had a wonderful time reading this notebook with its oily pages. We had to leave Iqaluit in the medical plane coming from Grise Fiord with Marcelline on board. As is often the case in the North, the plane was late. For five hours I was subjected to Dolly Parton's I Will Always Love You, played over and over in a van parked in a hangar, while Tommy sang along, not missing a word. It was past four a.m. when it occurred to me that Rosaire's gold reliquary had not been found after his death. The police had labelled and catalogued all the pieces of evidence found in the Arctic Circle's hotel room, but the mummified bit of his index finger wasn't there in the transparent bag the officer had handed me. I knew they had saved an Air France toothpick and an empty box of After Eight taken from a waste paper basket, and even a peach pit in plastic wrap found under the bed. All the rest seemed to have been scoured with a tooth brush dipped in industrial cleaner.

Sitting in the air-conditioned van, going through our ancestor's diary, I thought of the pine forest where my brother and I were born. We had grown up near Black Robe Lake, in the middle of very dense pine woods. The origins of the name are mysterious. Black Robes was the name once given by the Amerindians to the first French missionaries, who wore cassocks and came to convert them. But some think of the speckled trout, also garbed in black. Our lake was full of them. My uncle had bought these woods because his research indicated that Jean Nicolet's brother, a priest, had taught there for eight years. Over the threshold of our house there was a sign with the inscription: *Nicolet Manor, Ice Fishing*. Rudimentary huts adorned with spider webs, which we stored on shore over the summer, were moved onto the lake ice in December for the fishing. Every winter a real village, lit by gas lanterns, came to life: there one listened quietly to Céline Dion's songs, and tinsel twinkled until March. In every hut one made a hole in the ice with a drill, and the clients, warmed by alcohol, fished rainbow trout and brook trout. My father sent me into the kitchen at a very young age. The clients seemed to want only french fries. All the time. Non-stop, I carried paper cones from the house kitchen to the fishing huts. Rosaire was already doing public relations: he visited the clients, made them smile, and sometimes even sang Céline Dion's songs.

In summer, in the nearby pine woods, I gathered mushrooms that my mother put into the omelettes I adored. These wild mushrooms were my epiphany: they awakened my interest in cooking. Our husky had puppies, and my father showed me how to train them to hunt for the mushrooms. Every night I rubbed the mother's teats with matsutake, to sensitize the little ones to their odour. This mushroom was found in abundance where there was lichen in the pinewood, and it was much appreciated by the Japanese. My father would have liked us to market it. According to him, some expensive Japanese restaurants paid ten thousand dollars a kilo to season their rice with this cold-climate mushroom that smelled of pepper and cinnamon. Rosaire and I worked in the family business from the age of five, helping with the ice fishing in particular. At twenty we already had a long career behind us. But my father was never able to train us as he did the puppies.

We could have ensured the survival of the family tradition, but my brother and I decided to explore the world. Our father, who devoted his life to the huts, was a man of one vocation. What to do when you realize that you've been born to a man who has raised you with the sole idea of seeing you replace him in his tasks? We chose flight.

Rosaire was convinced of one thing: he was always right. He never hesitated to give me orders or tell me how to do something. He had a mission. His authoritarian side reassured me. With him, everything was going to turn out fine, while I had a cataclysmic temperament and always expected the worst. If there was no crate of endives in the Tuesday shipment I saw myself losing my job, because of course De Saxe Majolique probably hoped to be eating Belgian endives that evening, and nothing else. But my brother remained calm and rational, even in the tightest situations. When he went out at night to buy cigarettes, I had to stop myself from saying: "Look both ways before you cross the street!" His confidence did not stunt his generosity, he gave all he had to those he loved. As a child, in the shelters on the ice, he solved the Rubik's Cube for me and I went to proudly show it to my father, who gave me a hard slap on the back of the head to punish me for my vanity. Rosaire shared his talents. He kept nothing for himself. I sometimes had the feeling that my life took priority over his, despite our little childhood wars. I could count on him if I needed help. That made my life easier. For Rosaire, everything was possible, and together we would get out of any jam. I was sure he would never betray me. It was impossible for me to doubt him. This was a primary sensation that coursed through every fibre in my every muscle: my brother loved me. To make up for our parents' lack of feeling, we had created the solidest of bonds. This knot could not come undone. Many fraternal relationships are marked with jealousy and end up patched together, with life following its normal course towards indifference. Our closeness made relations with the outside less essential. Under the circumstances it was easier for me not to internalize, for now, the reality of my brother's death. I stubbornly, still, refused to mourn.

In the Inuit culture a man can choose to be reincarnated as a member of his family. It came to me that if I accepted Rosaire's utter disappearance, I would have to have a child with Marcelline. In that way I would ensure the reincarnation of my brother in our son, and live with the risk of having myself led by the nose.

13

A Man Jumps from a Plane

After a five-hour wait, I began to get worried about Marcelline. No one told us why the plane was late. A woman knocked on Tommy's fogged-over window and gave him a letter, shouting: "Are you going to Kimmirut? Will you give this to Marie-Perle?" When she walked off, I saw a baby's head peeking out of her fur coat. The air traffic controller then came up to us to say:

"I heard there was an accident over the glacial valley during the medical flight from Grise Fiord."

"Did the plane land safely?" Tommy asked at once, familiar with such situations.

"We don't have all the details," the controller replied.

I became hysterical.

"That's impossible, Tommy! We have to go there right away. Take me there. Marcelline is on board that flight, you... you know," I blurted out, stammering.

"There's no plane available, Ambroise," Tommy answered. "Calm yourself."

I took out the Dolly Parton cassette to get the radio, and we heard more details of the accident. A man had just jumped from the biplane while it was in full flight.

A man has jumped from a small plane not far from Grise Fiord, in Nunavut. Ac-

51

cording to police, a passenger on board a medevac flight, apparently in distress, forced open the airplane's door and jumped. The accident took place during a Sundog Air flight from Grise Fiord, a community in the north of Nunavut. At the time of the tragedy the plane was 180 kilometres from the Grise Fiord Airport, at an altitude of about seven kilometres. Bad weather is interfering with the investigation. A twin engine plane is conducting a search in the zone. A sergeant has informed the CBC that the searchers are relying on the GPS coordinates given them by the pilot. Police have not revealed the man's identity, but confirm that he was from Grise Fiord and that he suffered from depression, without giving any details on the reason for his presence on the medevac flight. The pilot of the plane in distress had signalled that there was an out-of-control passenger on board. The other passengers, after their forced return to Grise Fiord, have confirmed that a twenty-year-old man had opened the door and jumped, despite efforts by the two pilots to calm him down. Shaken by the accident, the two have refused any comment. A woman who was on board is apparently also missing.

The Director General of Sundog Air declared that his first thoughts were for the families of the victims. "We have been running flights out of Grise Fiord for at least thirty-five years, and there has never been a tragedy like this," he told the CBC.

According to a pilot, "enormous strength" would be required to open the exit door of a plane. "This door has four steel hinges that ensure the sealing of the main cabin to the fuselage. When the cabin is pressurized, it's impossible to open. There may have been a security failure." Minor damage to the cabin door was noted, according to the Transport Canada report.

The identity of the woman taken hostage by the man remains unknown. The police and the territorial coroner are presently looking into the case.

I turned off the radio, promising God that if Marcelline survived this fall, I would ask her to marry me as soon as I saw her.

14

Perlerorneq or the Weight of Life

We finally took a mine helicopter to return to Kimmirut early the next morning. I vomited into my tuque at least three times during the flight. We were carrying 244 cans of Campbell's cream of mushroom soup. On my return I wanted only one thing: news of Marcelline. But Brice de Saxe Majolique, Marxist gold panner, was waiting for me on the runway to ask if I could start work again that same day.

"Ambroise, the workers' bellies are the most important factor in the mine's morale. Eating is the main entertainment here. What you do is supremely important. It's impossible to replace you today," Brice declared grandly as he helped me out of the helicopter.

"Your workers eat nothing but apple turnovers. The dishwasher could easily take my place," I replied, tossing my soiled tuque onto the tarmac.

"Very funny, Ambroise. But I have no choice. Besides, and you know how refined my tastes are, I decided yesterday to ask for Marie-Perle's hand, and she accepted, so you can really exploit your talents as a chef. Your brother's death got me thinking. I want to love her until I die, and to marry her this summer. So between now and next Sunday, I want you to organize a grand banquet to celebrate our engagement, with scallops and raw sea urchins in their spiny shells, musk ox cheeks in a horseradish emulsion, snow goose eggs dusted with juniper powder, salmon tartare *royal* with sea coriander, all served up on stones and not on plates. I also want the guests to eat with their hands. I saw that in a restaurant in

Denmark, it's very fashionable. The drill foreman is getting engaged at the same time to an Inuit from Pond Inlet, and the rumour in the showers is that Tommy may propose to Marcelline sometime soon," Bryce shouted into my ears.

He held me by the neck, all the time yelling and leading me away from the propellers still spinning over our heads. I wanted to stick a shard of ice into his eye.

"You haven't heard? There was an accident on the medevac plane. Marcelline was on board," I cried.

"What are you talking about? I saw Marcelline coming out of her greenhouse less than ten minutes ago. Her strawberries will definitely be ripe for the banquet. She came back overnight, she wasn't on that flight. You invent more problems than you need."

I was relieved, but I thought that what Brice really deserved was that I cook him up a feast of lampreys prepared in fifty different ways. My heart was heavy. In the Inuit language, the word *perlerorneq* means "the burden of life." It refers to a deep depression caused by the dark winter. The symptoms vary: for instance, a woman can roll naked in the snow, or grab a knife and for no reason at all threaten her husband in their igloo. Anthropologists who have studied the question say that summer is not long enough to undo the effects of winter and the lack of outdoor activities. The absence of sun, the bitter cold of the preceding months, and all these upheavals were beginning to eat me away inside. There were violent impulses raging within me, but I got a grip on myself. I had imagined that Marcelline would be the first woman to touch the lead in my buttock without my reliving that first twinge, but in a few words Brice de Saxe Majolique had reminded me that I was a timid man, too tentative for what love required. Marcelline was alive, but my pledge to God was null and void.

And so I replied that my brother had just died and I had no intention of preparing the feast. I wanted to add that he looked ridiculous in his white Canada Goose coat because in Inuit culture that colour of coat was reserved for women. Once again, I held my tongue.

When I arrived in the kitchen Marcelline, the beautiful glaciologist, was talking to our new dishwasher, Kujjuk's cousin. Kujjuk still hadn't reappeared. Marcelline was saying there was no more sugar for coffee. When she turned to me, I replied, annoyed:

"There are jars of honey that look like teddy bears on the tables, that will do for sugar until tomorrow. This isn't the Ritz. The cargo plane arrives in twenty-four hours."

I tried not to raise my voice so I wouldn't startle my Inuit kitchen helper. The Inuit think you're crazy if you shout.

Marcelline, surprised to see me back from Iqaluit, looked sad. She murmured with uncharacteristic timidity:

"I'm sorry, Ambroise. I'm not trying to be difficult. I can't eat honey, I'm vegan."

Exasperated, Kujjuk's cousin answered for me:

"In my village, in Igloolik, they say that if a young woman likes to eat sugar, she'll have a husband who cheats on her."

"I have friends in Montreal who won't kiss a man who eats meat," Marcelline shot back, visibly vexed, before going right up to the dishwasher and telling him to his face that she never wanted a husband.

She then disappeared into the opening to the root cellar. The dull sound of her boots on the linoleum steps resonated in the staircase.

"You'll be very sorry, Marcelline, because I know someone who wants to marry you," said the Inuit, before turning to me.

I gestured to him to be quiet. My heart was pounding in my chest. But Marcelline had not heard.

To work in this difficult environment, you have to be tough, stronger than other women. Marcelline had to know how to assert herself with her eyes, and even to spit in the face of a new driver if he rubbed against her too insistently three times in the same week. In our small world where people are always in close quarters, bad relations between co-workers can easily degenerate. Marcelline had a sharp tongue. A sharp tongue and lilac eyes. Her smooth, thick black hair was like a panther's fur. Her cheeks were as pink and soft as the flesh of a fig. I hoped that the rumours circulating were false.

I decided to throw myself into my work right away. I had to start getting ready for the shellfish engagement party of Brice de Saxe Majolique and his gang. That might help erase the persistent image of my brother laid out in a bag in the middle of a refrigerated hangar. My new assistant showed me two big tubs with at least two hundred kilos of lobster and a hundred kilos of snow crabs to be cooked. Lobsters are cannibals, that's why we seal their claws with elastics to keep them from getting into fights where everyone would lose a leg. For me that was a perfect illustration of human relations at the mine.

The dishwasher tried to entertain me with his many tales about the notorious Iqaluit nightlife, claiming that he'd even had crabs in his eyelashes. I was removing lobster meat from their shells to make bisque and was listening to him with half an ear.

"You can even get chlamydia in your eyes if you're really creative," he said.

Fed up, I threw the shells into the dishwater.

"That's enough! This is not the time, and you shouldn't talk like that in front of Marcelline."

She was back up in the kitchen and didn't know in what corner to hide.

"I can defend myself fine on my own," she replied, before turning on her heels and heading for the cafeteria.

Scrubbing a waist-high pot with steel wool, the young Inuit had the last word:

"Marcelline has been very sweet since Tommy proposed to her. Women can't resist pilots, everybody knows that. Here, washing the white man's dishes, I don't have a chance," he pretended to blubber.

It seemed to me that Baffin Island had just sunk into the ocean. I went out. Far off, the employees' children were playing basketball on a rocky beach, on a plywood platform. They leaped around an enormous moon on the horizon, which seemed more part of the earth than of the sky. I made a wish: I asked my brother to protect me. I felt that he was not yet in the beyond, and that his soul was floating over Hudson's Bay, looking down on me.

15

Old Maid

If Marcelline married Tommy, she would trigger a tsunami of broken hearts in the mine. When Marcelline spoke, everyone hung on her every word. Her words buried themselves like moraines in my heart. To survive in the Arctic you have to tell great stories. Our only capital is our legends, skilfully contrived. Marcelline excelled in the art of storytelling. She loved to talk about her great grandfather, the painter Charles Tulley, who had created a canvas called *The Christmas Present*. A hymn to resilience, the image depicted in chiaroscuro a young girl with a white bonnet pulled down on her head. She had just been given a woodcutter's axe as a gift, and was proudly brandishing it with a hand that was missing a little finger. Marcelline's stories were irresistible.

They say that women can fall in love several times during their lifetimes, but for a man only one true love is possible. This love is harder for him to find and most often it occurs later in life. What comes before are often only friendships, games and conveniences that one takes for love. Since my arrival, I had the impression that all the women I'd known were of no consequence, that they were all pale copies of Marcelline. Was the air thinner in Kimmirut that my heart should be transformed into a pin cushion? She wouldn't be able to accept Tommy's proposal without me doing him in with my fillet knife. As a final despairing gesture I'd write her a farewell letter in mustard on the wall of my prison cell.

16

Arctic Kiwis

In this land of summers with no night and winters with no day, I was desperate to see Marcelline again to ask if she was really going to be engaged to Tommy. I also intended to explain to her what I thought of her and her diet. I wanted to know why she'd never talked to me about it before. It was eight-fifteen when she finally returned to the kitchen to take three kiwis from the cabinet that I'd carved with a paring knife so they'd look like roses. She was wearing little polar bears in her ears, carved in sea lion tusks by Kujjuk, and traditional snow goggles. I couldn't help saying:

"You know, it's not very ecological to eat vegan at the North Pole."

"No? Why?" she asked.

"Because vegetation is very rare here. You know, these kiwis were picked in New Zealand, where they were refrigerated and put on a boat to sail around the world. They passed through Montreal and took the plane to Iqaluit, to drop as air cargo right into your plate. If you think about my salary and the time it took me to transform them into delicate little roses, you could factor in an additional waste of resources. The mine doesn't care, because it has no choice but to treat you like royalty so you'll stick around. But the shipping cost for this fruit is astronomical. Every kiwi eaten here costs about forty dollars. Imagine the environmental footprint when you eat just one of these furry little fruits. Cabbages and watermelons cost the most because of their weight, but the mine doesn't give a damn. It's prepared to do anything to encourage the drillers and the specialized mechanics to stay here and not get scurvy. You like kiwis? Did you know that the Quebec language office, which doesn't like Anglicisms or New Zealand borrowings, wanted to rename the kiwi a 'vegetable mouse'"?

"That never occurred to me...," she replied, looking uncomfortable.

She was off balance. I'd gone for the jugular.

"It seems to me you ought to be the first to know. It's better to eat local. Fish from Pond Inlet, the char for example. That Arctic fish is a magnificent creature, and very good. They come in all colours: creamy white, silvery, pink, black, chrome yellow, orange. We get fish fillets in garbage bags every time a helicopter goes to fetch the polar bear monitors in their communities. Sometimes they come from Igloolik. We serve them raw at the table. That's how the Inuit workers like to eat. You can call it ceviche or gravlax or sashimi. As you wish. But at least you'll be at peace with your Greenpeace buddies. There's no overfishing here. And did you know that Arctic fish have an advantage over us? They secrete antifreeze proteins. When you eat them, you're protecting yourself from the cold."

Marcelline grimaced as if she were biting into a lemon. She didn't know what to say. She left the kitchen with her three kiwis, a bit frightened by my barely contained anger. I finished my shellfish bisque, a bilious taste at the back of my throat that gave me a dry cough. With the food processor full of shells, I couldn't hear what Marcelline was yelling as she turned around in the corridor, but it was easy to see that she was spitting fire.

17

The Presence of a Bear

In fact, Marcelline hoped that I'd croak so she could bury my head in the stoneware pot where she planted the sea samphire that seasoned her food all summer. At least that's what she told the dishwasher she ran into in the corridor. She was clearly furious.

All evening I asked myself the same question. I wondered if it was time for me to go back south, now that I was alone on the ice sheet. Nothing held me to Baffin Island any more. The sun was going to set in less than an hour. Outside, Tommy was amusing himself playing ball on the ice with the children of two drillers. He wore kneepads and jumped around with an energy I'll never have. I'm not very athletic, and to make myself attractive to women, I play the card of the tender and considerate man. Men like Tommy can get away with not knowing where the laundry basket is. They never do dishes unless they're guilty of making a gaffe and are looking for some way of being excused. I've always thought that if I didn't participate in all these household chores women wouldn't love me any more, that I'd become useless in their eyes.

A thick fog lifted while they were playing soccer with their ball, made in part from narwhal guts, which bring good luck, according to the Inuit. The sun continued its descent. Far off, I suddenly spotted a scrawny polar bear, its fur very yellow, approaching the players. I didn't say anything, just kept watch out of the corner of my eye. It had come to inspect the unknown object bouncing around on the ice. Fascinated by the ball, it started to chase it among the dumbfounded players, who quickly dispersed to return to camp. Nothing in the world makes you feel so alive as being in the presence of a bear.

I felt sad. I would never have the chance to describe this scene to my brother; it would have made an impression during a fishing trip or on a hunt. A specialist in treaties and ancestral deeds, Rosaire also liked to hunt polar bears. He venerated them. They were his passion. But he played the taxidermist with them as well, which was more dangerous. Polar bear trophies are outlawed in the United States and Europe, but they're still tolerated in Canada, where trophy hunters must, however, pay the price. A black market exists, of course, especially among Russian oil billionaires. Even if he was mainly busy with the circumpolar affairs of the Canadian government, and on occasion those of Brice de Saxe Majolique, during the nine last months, Rosaire had been working on the Nunavut Constitution to help the Inuit achieve immunity from endangered species laws.

Lost in thought, I had not seen Tommy approach. Suddenly I heard him say, out of breath:

"How could you just sit there without warning us of the danger?"

"I didn't see the bear right away," I lied. "I was studying the sun's trajectory on the horizon. Optical phenomena have started to interest me now that my life has no more meaning."

"Rosaire once said to me: 'When someone harms you, he's asking you to show him more love.'"

Tommy was waxing philosophical all of a sudden.

I went to lie down but I couldn't sleep. For the first time since the death of my brother, and despite my fatigue of recent days, I took time to reflect. There was a lot at play in Rosaire's death. I should, like everyone else, have been pinning my brother's murder on the short-tempered Lumi. But deep in my insomnia, something was making me suspect Brice de Saxe Majolique.

18

Arctic Disenchantment

The antler is a moose's weapon, it uses it to defend itself. Rosaire, for his part, didn't know how to protect himself from his enemy. He was drawn, despite himself, to what was unlawful. The dark side of my brother's life was his trafficking in taxidermy. He practised this illegal activity as if it were a hobby. He helped native people exploit their ancestral rights for commercial ends, which was prohibited. They had the right to hunt, but could not sell the products that they hunted. It's well known that those who admit to no shameful little secrets are the ones who harbour the most sordid stories. The vilest tragedies take place in the most beautiful places. I knew that my brother had sold polar bears to Brice de Saxe Majolique back when he was still a taxidermist in Paris.

Brice de Saxe Majolique often seemed to make bad choices when he arrived at a crossroads. To cater to his love of hunting, he'd bought a taxidermy business in Paris, The Golden Calf. An accomplished hunter of red foxes and ducks, he had always dreamed of bringing down a snowy owl in the middle of the night, a sly and elegant beast that he saw for the first time at the Paris Book Fair. The animal on display wore a pink tutu to attract passers-by and to tempt them to leaf through a book on birds of prey written by a man from Igloolik who had an iron rule: "One book signed, one finger of whiskey." The owl, perched on the leather-gloved arm of a young Inuit woman, emitted a long "hoohoohoo," its throat shaken by a spasm. Seeing Brice de Saxe Majolique, it lowered its head and suddenly tried to attack. Fortunately, the night raptor had its wings slightly clipped, and was tied with a leather thong to its mistress, or the taxidermist prince would have received its talons full in his face. Brice de Saxe Majolique spent hours in front of the young Inuit named Lumi, looking the beast in the eyes: big round eyes, yellow, the eyes of a killer. This experience is what decided him to do business in French America, which would prove to be an ideal playing field for the prince.

But Brice was soon disillusioned. Lumi had never imagined he would travel all that way to see her. She liked to go out Saturday nights to Iqaluit's cavernous bars. She liked to vomit into the snow. She didn't want to spend weekends by the fire listening to Brice de Saxe Majolique reading her aloud excerpts from his family tree. She wanted to eat standing up, right out of a can, without silverware, without a plate for her bread. After their separation, Lumi decided to go and study in Montreal. She was taking her life into her own hands.

De Saxe Majolique had left the damp comfort of his private mansion in Paris for a snowmobile adventure in a white inferno. His passion for Lumi had been the trigger: he hunted in tights, English style, with a flask over his shoulder made from an elk's stomach. His faithful hound wore a snug little wool-lined coat in matching tartan, and snow boots. The taxidermist prince lived off his private wealth and had not cancelled his subscription to the *Annuaire de la noblesse de France*, whose volumes accumulated on the doormat in front of his Paris apartment.

Brice de Saxe Majolique had set off for North America at peace with himself, convinced that France was restricting his freedom. Hemmed in by traditions and family obligations, he told one of his incredulous cousins: "I will explore the Arctic Circle. There you can find everything, except what we have here." He was persuaded that to abandon his mother country was to launch himself into life. No one was going to force him to start a family in order to perpetuate his line, dote on his children and live a life he abhorred. He wanted to become what no one expected of him.

Although born into idleness, Brice labored like someone from the lower classes when he arrived in North America. It was in part to impress Lumi, who remained indifferent to him. He was a ski lift operator in Tremblant for two seasons, helping American ladies in sheared mink coats to settle in their seats, cigarettes between their lips. At the time, he wore a fluorescent green one-piece Le Coq ski suit with full-length zippers. He soon got rid of it, as such garb was more appropriate to the slopes at Chamonix than to the cold Canadian winters.

After Lumi's rejection, Brice de Saxe Majolique bought a claim, a mining exploration title. He began to work as a prospector at Kimmirut and he went to Iqaluit, to the Arctic Circle bar, every Tuesday around noon. However, the town repelled him, because it prevented him from burying himself in weighty rumination. Since the loss of Lumi, Brice de Saxe Majolique had pain in his liver, and his skin had yellowed. He ogled the dancers in their thigh-high boots and rainbow-coloured plastic nails. A Russian from Volgograd was his favourite: she writhed above him on her long spiked heels, did the splits a thousand times over and scoured his eardrum with her tongue, before straddling him, her legs over the back of his chair. He sometimes pushed her away violently. His challenge now was to protect his body from harmful sentimental intrusions. As if he was surrounded by invisible barbed wire. Before leaving the Arctic Circle bar, he always paid a long visit to the toilet, cleaning his hands with a cloth he kept in his pocket and a few drops of antibacterial soap.

At the time, Brice de Saxe Majolique was a chronic victim of ancestral melancholia, and he couldn't stop himself, it seemed, from reacting violently to his ingrained sadness. He had tried, in the past, after downing two bottles of fortified wine, to kill himself by spraying insecticide on his tongue. He came to with a monster headache and ethanol breath.

But when Lumi reappeared in the region alongside Rosaire, Brice de Saxe Majolique's dire torment seemed suddenly to abate.

"Rosaire is the perfect man for her," he told me one day, leaning on the bar.

I remember thinking that when you are lied to with such aplomb, you always feel the person talking is trying to dupe you. You have to either follow your instincts or believe in the lie.

Lying in my bed with a Nunavut flag wrapped around my head to block out the midnight sun, I told myself that Brice had poisoned my brother, hoping to cast the blame on Lumi.

19

A Bunch of Thin Asparagus

I got a surprise when I walked into the cafeteria that Friday morning. Mitsy Cooper was waiting for me. She'd arrived early by helicopter, and wanted my opinion on Rosaire's murder. Taking a mouthful of an apple turnover she was holding in one hand and inhaling her cigarette with the other, Mitsy showed me a video of Lumi's interrogation, obtained semi-legally, on her phone. Despite my doubts about her working methods, I was curious to see the video.

Lumi had been taken to the Iqaluit police station after my brother's body was discovered. In the North, there is a lot of violence, many suicides, marital disputes and ample drug trafficking, but murders are rather rare. The police have to find the guilty party quickly to show that they are competent. The officer on duty that day seemed delighted: he would be alone with this beautiful native woman to question her. In the interrogation room, a little pink plastic crucifix was nailed to the wall. It fell to the ground while the policeman was reading Lumi her rights.

Right away, she said:

"I don't need a lawyer, I didn't do anything. Ask me whatever you want."

"You were the last person to see Rosaire alive. Did you kill him?"

"No. He was dead when I came into the room. I'd spent the night at home."

"How did Rosaire die?"

"Are you crazy or what? Now I want to speak to a lawyer."

"You don't want to continue the interview and cooperate with the police? It would go better for you if you did. Otherwise judicial procedures will kick in, and everything's slow here. It could take years... Lawyers drop in once a month, by plane. You know Bearskin Airlines? The waiting list is long."

"I love Rosaire, I didn't kill him. I wanted to live my life with him."

"Rosaire was not your boyfriend. You were only one girl on his list, along with others. Talk, because you'll be locked up in prison if you don't tell the truth."

"I have the right to see a lawyer."

"You'll rot for two months in a cold prison cell, if you want to wait to see a lawyer here."

"Let me take a lie detector test," cried Lumi.

"Usually, those who ask for a lie detector test are guilty."

The officer smiled, proud of his answer. He then left Lumi alone in the interrogation room for four hours. She wasn't reacting like a woman who had just lost her loved one, but like someone on the defensive. In her Lululemon slacks, she started to assume yoga positions, like the dolphin and the warrior. If Mitsy hadn't been by my side, I would have watched the four hours of video with her alone in the room, to analyze all her movements. Lumi's answers had struck me as improvised, but calculated.

When the officer reappeared, Lumi had her arms crossed and her head on the table. She asked him for a coffee. He went up to her and stroked her side, inching towards her breast.

"You're used to selling your favours to men. I know who you are, Lumi."

"I'm not guilty of anything more than having three drinks of whiskey with Rosaire at the Arctic Circle last night. He'd come in from Montreal and had brought me a bunch of thin asparagus he'd bought at an organic farm over the weekend. He even had me taste one..."

Lumi suddenly seemed disoriented and not so sure of herself. Tired. Then the policeman left the room, to only return two hours later. Without coffee. Mitsy advanced the video.

Lumi was visibly exhausted. She held her head in her hands.

"Everyone knows your father is a white man, a Finn who'd come here on a scientific expedition. But your mother hid it from you until you were

eighteen. Do you really think I'm going to have sympathy for a Métis?"
It was at that precise moment that the video cut out.

20

Puikartuq or Surfacing to Breathe

I felt very grateful to Mitsy. But since seeing the video, I could no longer stay put. I knew that in the North you had to adapt. Some caterpillars have to keep growing for fourteen consecutive years before getting big enough to become moths.

I adjust poorly. I'm someone comforted by routine. My anxiety is my greatest handicap. I even have trouble performing the most ordinary acts of survival, such as inhaling and exhaling. I breathe in at irregular intervals like whales that surface every twenty minutes. At night, sleeping, I sometimes forget to breathe out, as though I have apnea. My torso expands, expands, expands, until I wake with a start.

Panting and wheezing as if in need of an asthma inhaler, pulling a wooden sled loaded with an order of a hundred and forty-four frozen cod, I had a revelation. It was clear that Lumi had lied. Monday May 3, in Iqaluit, the day of my brother's death, there was a municipal election. According to a Nunavut decree, no alcohol consumption is allowed in bars forty-eight hours before a vote, at risk of a fine. Lumi said on the video that she'd had three whiskeys with Rosaire at the Arctic Circle on Sunday night, the day before the election. So was she lying?

In my mind, I couldn't stop running a loop of all the information Mitsy had given me. I was very impressed by her involvement in this matter, while the police seemed to be twiddling their thumbs. During her research she had discovered that three days before his death, Rosaire had cancelled the million dollar life insurance policy he'd taken out as an engagement present for Lumi. She had also found the copy of a receipt indicating that on May 3rd, at 8:39 a.m., he had mailed an envelope addressed to my apartment in Montreal, a lodging I'd kept to store all my belongings. I'd arrived in Kimmirut with just my knapsack. It was hard to know whether this piece of mail was still in the hold of a twin-engine crossing the tundra. The route between postal code X0A 0H0 and the South is strewn with take-offs and landings. The envelope might have a lot to say about the murder motive.

The pathologist, a wet blanket in a three-quarter length platinum-coloured Kanuk coat, had finally arrived in Iqaluit. He'd performed the autopsy during the night and had missed his plane for Montreal, which had made him furious. Mitsy phoned me late that afternoon to give me his verdict, while I was extracting cod cheeks to make a soup. He had found a toxic concentration of Vitamin A in Rosaire's liver, and had concluded that he was poisoned, though he couldn't say how without a laboratory analysis. Rosaire's body would be flown to Montreal. It was the first case of the sort that he'd seen.

In my opinion, there were many trails that could be followed. Rosaire was known for his widespread love affairs. Many women had become radioactive in his company and could have easily been capable of poisoning him. What was needed was proof. His Montreal apartment was being searched. Also, a container of Canadian Tire antifreeze was found in Lumi's pickup truck. American women often used it to get rid of their husbands, as its sweet taste is similar to that of energy drinks like Red Bull.

I was having trouble concentrating on preparations for the engagement banquet. Every move I made seemed mechanical. I was suffering. My heart was mush. I had to prepare musk-ox marrow, but all I had in my head was a list of Rosaire's potential female enemies. He had a special magnetism, a self-assurance that made women who came within a metre of him unsteady on their feet. In his orbit, I too was calmed by his serenity.

His work as a lawyer for the mine was controversial too, as was, in fact, his research on Jean Nicolet, our illustrious ancestor who had found the Chinese mappemonde discrediting Christopher Columbus. My brother's conclusions had infuriated a small community of scholars who had spent their lives as researchers studying Columbus. Rosaire was treated as a fabulist, a revisionist, even a forger. I felt very much alone in this maelstrom. There were so many trails and so few solutions. I suddenly realized that my cod looked like it had been filleted by a madman. I dumped the carnage in a plastic basin and put it out for the wolfhounds, who began to yap so loudly they could be heard for kilometres. The leader of the pack bit my ankle and threw me to the ground, pulling on my pant leg. I got up, brushed the ammonia-scented snow off my coat and walked to the sea, teary-eyed. I tried to understand why Lumi had lied. I had never seen her drink whiskey; she preferred coloured cocktails made with Marie Brizard. The sky over the glacial spur was the colour of a bruise, and two narwhals were knocking their tusks together, like musketeers wielding their swords, far off, in Hudson's Bay.

21

The Isometry of Love

Lumi's lie tormented me all day. An entire day, during which I extract-
ed the coral from a hundred and forty-nine langoustines to make bis-
cuits, prepared birch syrup and a beet granita, kneaded liquorice bread,
and used the flesh of the scarlet langoustines to prepare an algae-fla-
voured tartare for the feast the next day. They say that you should keep
your friends close and your enemies even closer. And so I spread caviar
as grey as a gun barrel onto cubes of raw char, and brought it to Tommy, who was playing Nintendo on the TV screen in the cafeteria. I took
the opportunity to ask him what he thought of Lumi. He explained that
Lumi was a good girl, even if she hadn't had an ordinary life. Then he
talked about her beginnings:

"Lumi means 'snow' in Finnish. They say that her father was a white
explorer born in Pori, Finland. She came into the world in a cabin
perched on a cliff called 'Narwhal Bay' in Inuktitut," he told me, as if in
a trance.

"Narwhal Bay... Rosaire adored narwhals. He spoke to me often about
this legendary animal. In Christian times it was thought to be the myth-
ical unicorn, because of its spiral tusk and its timidity. It was called the
unicorn of the seas."

"The Narwhal's tusk is actually a long twisted tooth," Tommy went
on. "The Inuit made the celebrated muktuk from it, a gastronomic dish
prepared from the animal's skin and a thick slice of fat that tastes of ha-

zelnuts. I must be one of the few Inuit who don't like *muktuk*," he added, laughing and tapping like a lunatic on his console. "I prefer seal pie or caribou pizza."

"Inuit children adore muktuk, almost as much as candy!" I replied, avidly downing a spoonful of Arctic caviar. "But I understand you. For me, it's like a plate of offal I once ate in a Lyon tavern: breaded tripe. It was just a huge serving of fat!"

I went back to the kitchen, numb with concern, to prepare a terrine of rabbit with lovage. The young dancer who had charmed Rosaire's heart was facing serious accusations. I knew her lifestyle had distanced her from the community these last years. I couldn't resist distracting Tommy from his game a second time.

"It's as if Lumi had several lives. She's experienced incredible things for a young girl born in the Arctic darkness," I said, after a long silence.

"The moon didn't set for the eighteen days following her birth, and her mother predicted that was the sign of a catastrophe to come," replied Tommy, his voice slightly hoarse.

I'd never confessed to Rosaire that I'd known Lumi long before him, in a brothel in Old Montreal. The day when he introduced me to his future fiancée, I saw in her eyes that she remembered me too, but that our secret would be kept intact. I didn't even blink. She remained calm. I kissed her cheeks. We never needed to talk about it. We never spoke of it in his absence, out of respect for my brother. The law of silence that prevailed at the brothel seemed to take precedence over all other societal dictates, scrupulously inscribed in books of law and ratified by men in wigs. Our common aim was to not hurt my brother, and we protected him with our silence until the day he died. I never wanted to disappoint Rosaire. But today I know I was wrong to keep the secret.

I have to say that though Lumi fascinated me, I never loved her. I was afraid of her and her power to cast spells. I was above all spellbound by her story, which she told so adroitly. Like her ancestors, hunters of belugas, finbacks, and narwhals, she seemed unafraid to move through the night, even on ice, and loved to repeat certain details out of her past, as though forging a legend. In this land of Nunavut, the best storytellers always survived longer than the others.

22

The Judges' Spice

Lumi had told me her story so many times, those nights when we drank a bit too much, that I owed it to myself to find the incongruous detail that would reveal to me the truth about my brother's death. Alone in the kitchen, freeing two hundred dozen scallops from their shells, I was cursing under my breath. While separating salsify roots from their leaves, which I let fall into a pail, I ran through her story in my head.

She'd forgotten to say that she had gone south to get away from Brice de Saxe Majolique. She preferred to claim that, younger, she loved the city's existential excitement, the public transportation, the colours of the Montreal Metro. She was fascinated by the young men modelling their wardrobes after the hero of *American Psycho*. In the city, she felt like a prey. She hung out with Whites. She never really felt at home anywhere.

Lumi often told me that at university, she envied her fresh-faced friends, whose only concern was to have fun. They got together in bars, went to punk rock shows and read melancholic poets who prolonged their childhood. A whole new world opened up to her, she whose life had always been subject to the day-to-day constraints required to survive in the North. In the southern city, she wrote her schedule with a ball-point pen on the palm of her hand, but arrived late to class. She was often exhausted, she yawned, she stared out the window. She slept for an hour at home, then left for work. Lumi had to work every weekend to pay for her education. She had always preferred work to idleness. The idea of vacations was foreign to her. She only took them at Chrismas, Easter and on the Queen's birthday. She missed two things: seeing the procession of Baffin Sea icebergs as big as jade cathedrals, and having her suitors carve whale calves in talc as an amorous rite.

It was Marie-Perle, a tall blonde with shadows under her eyes, corseted into her leather zipped coat, who approached her. She spoke to Lumi in front of a university building, smoking a cigarette between two cracks of pink chewing gum. It was right away a question of work. Marie-Perle had traded her favours for money, replying to messages online from students seeking a soulmate, but it had become too dangerous. Now she worked as a receptionist at a red light place, and was in love with a former client called Rosaire. Lumi's meeting with Marie-Perle threw her into a shady world that had been totally foreign to her. Life, finally, would stop eluding her, or so she thought.

Located near the law courts, the brothel catered to a clientele made up largely of lawyers, coroners, and clerks of the court. The place was lit by a thousand candles, the salon walls were covered in ancient wallpaper whose red background was decorated with blue and green parrots perched on yellow-orange hibiscuses. It was a friendly place, and very theatrical. On the street and at university, the girls dressed like everyone else, in severe glasses and jeans, but within the red light walls they were laced into ivory corsets, adorned with luminous jewellery in gold filigree and walked as though on stilts, in high heels with red soles. From a slight distance you would have thought you were at a great Venetian orgy painted by Canaletto.

In her high-pitched voice, Marie-Perle convinced Lumi to try it for at least a night. Despite her recruiter's counselling, Lumi didn't know what to expect from her first client. With no elaborate outfit, she chose to wear something she had bought in a second-hand shop: a moss green silk dress from the 1920s, with a beige butterfly woven into the collar. She was offered a glass of wine, which she quickly gulped down. One of the girls said to her: "A woman of the world never touches the bowl of the glass. She takes it by the stem." She was a bit afraid of being beaten up, of returning home with swollen eyes, her nose encrusted with blood and her dress in shreds. Nothing of the sort happened. Her first client was a forty-year-old professor with greying temples. He wore a blue Italian suit, a powder-blue linen shirt, and caramel leather shoes. He was more attentive than any of the men she'd known before. They spent more time talking than anything else. He taught Scandinavian literature at the university. He was interested in the endangered cultures of various Arctic countries and said he was preparing a study on Shor culture. Only ten thousand people in the world still speak Shor, a language from the south of Russia built on Finnish and Turkish roots. He was very excited, because he had just laid hands on a book of poetry written by Gennady Kostochakov, called *I am the Last Shor Poet,* and he hoped to interview him for the *Cahiers des littératures arctiques.* Internal conflicts in Russia had dispersed the small population groups that still spoke this language, hastening its extinction.

Lumi emerged from the house utterly astonished, almost stunned, but filled with happiness and with fast money in her pocket. With her five hundred dollars she bought a red salmon-skin billfold in which to keep the money she would use to pay for her university education. She wouldn't have to go back to the Arctic for a long time. All her problems seemed solved.

Lumi would become a girl you paid for her company, and she promised herself that she would keep this secret locked in her heart for the rest of her life. It was an exchange of favours: she consoled businessmen with her northern beauty, and they talked about things unknown to her, travel in countries she would never visit. The world passed before her eyes, and thanks to their confidences she learned to understand it. She came to know truths she would find nowhere else.

The following days, Lumi met even more dazzling clients, such as the doctor for the Montreal Opera Company. He was paid to attend performances and ensure that there was a medical presence on site. He took the pulse of the young singers. During each act there were at least two elderly ladies overcome by the heat for him to revive, weighed down by their jewels, with rings like Turkish eels on every finger Lumi was an opera lover and drank in the stories the doctor brought to her. In 1992 he had seen Wagner's *Ring of the Nibelung* six nights in a row, because one of his colleagues couldn't bear to hear "The Ride of the Valkyries" one more time.

One night, Marie-Perle, who had become her friend, asked her to stay for a while with Rosaire, the young lawyer she was seeing, and to answer the phone while she went to fetch sushi. Rosaire, at that point, liked to spend time with uncomplicated working girls like Marie-Perle. He easily seduced women who lived for beauty above all, and sought a man like him. That was a luxury I had never had.

Rosaire, sitting on the couch beside Lumi, immediately started talking about Iqaluit. He had been there for work. Against all expectations, Lumi fell head over heels for Rosaire. He asked her to close her eyes and then secretly wrote his phone number on the flyleaf of one of the books on the shelf along the wall of the corridor. He told Lumi that she had to find the right book among the hundred titles on the shelves. Lumi was dazzled. Marie-Perle, when she came back, sensed that something had happened, but said nothing.

Lumi spent two days looking for the book. She had to be discreet, and only conducted her search when there was no one in the room. Rosaire had chosen Herodotus' *Histories*. She phoned him immediately. He confessed that he'd been waiting for her call ever since he'd written down his number. Since their meeting, he'd thought only of her.

Rosaire began to see Lumi every Wednesday. In those days, she applied golden glitter to her eyelids. Marie-Perle had her day off on Wednesday, and always had lunch with her mother at Pinocchio, an Italian restaurant.

In a few weeks, Lumi had already learned more at the brothel than in all her readings of Nietzsche. She felt free. For a woman who had drunk at the same spring as a herd of caribou all her life, her new experiences were life-changing. She now understood how physical attraction was based on the distance between bodies. She saw why we all wish for novelty in our long monogamous relationships. Lumi often said that we're tempted by what we do not know, by what is foreign to us, because we don't understand it. She now knew why secret brothels made fortunes.

As she sat in the salon with the other girls, waiting for the phone to ring, Lumi talked about prehistoric art in the Bering Strait and the birth of contemporary Inuit art in the 1950s, which was, she said, to fill the white peoples' need for soapstone sculptures. The red light girls like her were educated, which pleased their clients. Her anthropology professor had explained to her the meaning of the old expression, *the judges' spice*:

it was another way of saying "bribe." The girls were in the good graces of the judges and lawyers who worked at the law courts and didn't have to worry about the police. On the contrary, these gentlemen all brought them stylish presents. They were snowed under by the scent of lilies and the garish colours of birds of paradise. Marie-Perle, who hid a spoon and a little bag of cocaine under the bathroom sink, had received from a judge who was one of her regular clients for two years, a pink gold charm bracelet in the form of a swan, which everyone envied her.

Every night Lumi asked herself how normal men, charming and amorous, were able to return home and embrace their sleeping children, after bestowing so much affection on a stranger whom they paid. It was as if she were at last seeing the other side of the picture: her experience provided her with a clear-sighted view of domestic relations, but her confidence in men was forever shaken. She had the answer to the question that all women must ask themselves. But it wasn't what most women wanted to hear. Deep down, they knew that they were being betrayed, but they chose to do nothing to protect the house and the silver. Perhaps it would have been better if Lumi had never been exposed to the other side of that coin. She could have gone on, like everyone else, eyes shut, towards the light at the end of the tunnel, sheltered from reality.

Sometimes Lumi imagined the other girls, much older, telling stories of their gold-digging days for the hundredth time, and she doubted that would be much to live for. For her, meanwhile, a humdrum life was not enough. She hesitated for a long time before embarking on an affair with Rosaire. Her glittery eye shadow left tell-tale traces on him, and Marie-Perle began to suspect something. One day she spotted a gold sparkle, almost invisible, on Rosaire's forehead. It was a Wednesday night, at dinner time. At first Marie-Perle didn't think much of it. She told herself that there had to be an explanation. Rosaire must have paid a visit to his office storeroom for some paper, and this brilliant bit of glitter had fallen from the box that held the office's Christmas decorations. She told herself that three times over, to persuade herself. She noted other strange signs but said nothing, opting for denial, a more untroubled state of mind than that of suspicion. Something intrigued her though: when she got into Rosaire's car the front passenger seat always seemed positioned for someone shorter than she was. Marie-Perle was a five-foot-nine liana, and had to push the seat all the way back when she was in the vehicle with Rosaire.

The day she saw some glitter on his neck, she let drop her naïve scenario. She began to suspect a secretary at the law office. And so she started to have lunch with Rosaire regularly, except on Wednesdays, which she spent with her mother. But she was able to ascertain that none of the women working with him wore that kind of makeup.

This is how the mysterious transfer of gold dust really took place. Every Wednesday morning the name of Rosaire's law office appeared on the brothel's display. Rosaire made an appointment with Lumi for eleven o'clock. The replacement receptionist was discreet, and did not enter their appointment into the register. Lumi applied her iridescent eye shadow, "champagne sheen," and pink lip gloss. When she knew that Rosaire was coming she felt like an teenager again, as if she were waiting for her first little boyfriend in a puffy dress, her deer antler bracelet on her wrist, on the way to the graduation dance. When he arrived, she pretended not to notice, to be busy. One of the girls brought Rosaire to the dungeon room and told him to make himself comfortable. The girls called the room at the end "the dungeon," because the wall behind the bed was stone, and they were never able to heat it properly.

When at last she burst into the room, Rosaire was naked, lying on his stomach. It was as if a mutation then took place, and for an hour they became one. Even if he paid her, it was Lumi who was attracted to him. Awe and desire merged in her eyes. Lumi felt as if she were having her way with him. Afterwards, she sat on him and he wept a little. She talked to him then about winter skies in the Arctic, which resembled the mother of pearl in the hollow of a seashell.

When I met Lumi that first time, which would remain our secret, she told me about the Fata Morgana: those Arctic mirages caused by the refraction of the sun's rays on cold mornings, painting pictures of non-existent mountain ranges in the glacial air. They had even, at times, been mapped by sailors. She told me that the Fata Morgana proved that nothing is truly real, and that the rational is but a figment of the European imagination.

Lumi's new education had taught her that there was a significant difference between the two sexes' perception of reality. Lumi knew that men wanted to linger in bed for hours, and that women wanted to come as fast as possible, on the edge of a table, as if to get things over with. Lumi would remember for the rest of her life the scent of a black candle that burned in the "dungeon" while she was with Rosaire. She often thought that if they had been married, she'd have started to hate him and feel contempt for him after a few years, because she would have assumed control in every domain. In the end, if she were married to Rosaire, she'd have had no choice but to suppress her instincts. But there, in that place, their romantic dream was preserved in an intoxicating first time that renewed itself again and again.

One noon hour, Rosaire offered Lumi a little hibiscus with orange flowers. After his rendezvous with her, Marie-Perle was waiting for him at the corner under a street lamp. That day, Lumi's makeup had not shed itself onto his skin, but Rosaire had to promise never to see her again. Marie-Perle never admitted to him that she had discovered everything thanks to a speck of gold glitter. It was her secret way of finding out whether he would keep his word.

A few months after Marie Perle found out what had been going on, Rosaire moved to Iqaluit to work with the Canadian government on maritime jurisdiction over the Lomonosov Ridge.

Lumi prudently chose to return to the North with Rosaire. She packed her bags and had a hard time leaving the South. "I miss the trees," she observed after the first week. To avoid dying of boredom, she insisted on working at the Arctic Circle, making for violent quarrels between her and Rosaire.

Finally, it was her desire to find Rosaire again that led Marie-Perle to Iqaluit. The relations between the three of them remained ambiguous, consisting of polite smiles, unspoken hatred and cold looks. The two best friends had become rivals, but I could not make myself believe that Lumi killed my brother. It seemed impossible to me.

23

The Garden of Miracles

Tommy had fallen asleep over his video game, and two teens passing behind him, laughing, lifted off his John Deere cap. In the Arctic, only 30% of the people are women. Close relationships do occur, some become marriages, but most end in a return air trip. What Rosaire felt for Lumi was very different, and he hoped for only one thing: for his feelings to be reciprocated. Nothing was less certain though after the Inuit beauty returned to Iqaluit and was hired at the Arctic Circle. It seemed like she blamed my brother for forcing her to leave the South. Her games with the soldiers seemed like acts of revenge. After a few months, she may have hoped that Rosaire would propose. Was she afraid that he would remain a womanizer?

Some Inuit, especially those in Iqaluit, often order in Filipino mail-order brides who covet Canadian citizenship. To them, spending five years with a husband who may be alcoholic and eats muktuk or seal in a treeless land at the heart of an endless night lasting six months seems like a fair bargain. They think it's the best way to acquire a semblance of North American freedom. But Arctic love matches often consist of outsized desires and disillusionments.

For my part, I was not the only one to covet Marcelline. In this arid and solitary landscape, the geologists all seemed to hanker after her, trying to seduce her with their knowledge of paleoclimatology in extreme Arctic fossil forests or the Paleolithic tribes. I suspected that even Brice de Saxe Majolique wanted to charm her, particularly with his mycological knowledge. One day as I was passing in front of the miracle greenhouse, I saw Tommy snoring in a corner of a big velvet couch covered in yellow roses. Brice de Saxe Majolique was sitting at the little white wrought iron table, leafing through a catalogue of wild mushroom species in the Arctic.

"This catalogue will help me to save lives, because at least two people die every year from mushroom poisoning," I heard him say, guileful as always.

Marcelline was spraying the leaves of her scrawny plants, and didn't seem at all impressed.

Even if he'd saved Rosaire's life once, I often wanted to poison my boss.

I have to confess that I was sometimes blinded by jealousy. The previous winter, on a night when the thermometer showed sixty degrees below Celsius, I saw from a great distance a man and a woman on the shore behind Violet Rock, gazing at the sea. I thought I recognized the silhouettes of Tommy and Marcelline. The pilot had stretched Marcelline out on the flat rock to kiss her, and he had taken the time to light the wick of a little fireworks display planted in the snow. In my opinion this whole business was very dangerous, because at that temperature skin exposed to the air freezes in less than three minutes. The pyrotechnic display exploded into a fuchsia heart and started a small fire in a stretch of lichen. Amid the sugary, resinous odour, I saw Tommy kissing Marcelline. Their breath blew out from between their lips, forming ribbons of vapour that rose skywards. It was the first time I'd seen a man and a woman kissing at sixty degrees below zero. The effect was more spectacular than an aurora borealis. I'm certain that they were risking hypothermia.

At first I was furious. Back in my kitchen, I poured a little cooking port into a coffee cup and hit the granite counter so hard with my hand that the ring on my little finger smashed to bits, the one I'd had Kujjuk make for Marcelline . The shock left me with a little red blood blister on the finger.

24

The Lomonosov Ridge

Up at dawn, I was in the cafeteria with Brice de Saxe Majolique. Lifting his nose from his paper while I was shoving three industrial-sized sheets of apple turnovers into the oven, he shouted:

"You know what, Ambroise? I have the same measurements as Lance Armstrong, five foot eight and a hundred and sixty-five pounds!"

I sighed and said nothing. I was half-watching Mitsy Cooper on TV. For once, she was addressing more important issues than my brother's dubious lifestyle. The issue was Arctic sovereignty, and the story concerned an *Igloolik inukshuk*, an Inuit stone sculpture representing a man. It had been covered in caribou graffiti by teens during the night. Misty announced, in a tinny voice:

> A group of Canadian and Danish experts have declared Canada's sovereignty in the Arctic, one of the last unexplored regions on earth. The Lomonosov Ridge is the orphan everyone is fighting over. The Canadians have been able to prove that this underwater mountain range is attached to the North American continent. For their part, the Russians, who have planted a flag in the ocean's depths, wrongly claim that the Ridge is part of the Eurasian continent.
>
> For the weather, here is tomorrow's forecast: Inlet: 0; Iqaluit: 6; Yellowknife: 10.
>
> Finally, in some surprising news, the first pietà sculpture in North

Polynya

America was found yesterday in Iqaluit. This curious message was written on its base: "The Chinese discovered America."

It was the same sentence that had been scrawled on my brother's forearm. I knew right away that I had to talk to Mitsy. I had to see this pietà. I tried to reach her by phone, but she wasn't answering her cell. I suddenly remembered that she was still on the air.

Mitsy had lived in Iqaluit for ten years, more exactly since the birth of Nunavut, the moment when French, once compulsory according to Canadian law, ceased to be taught as a second language in schools. Mitsy's first report had dealt with the refusal of Canada Post to shorten Nunavut to NU (naked in French), because it was judged to be too immodest.

I absolutely had to see her, to learn more. I wasn't starting work again until Saturday night, when I'd be overseeing final preparations for the next day's banquet. I left immediately, without a second thought, in Tommy's plane. As was so often the case, he was going to pick up a shipment of tools in Iqaluit. He had to ask me my weight, to be sure that the twin engine wouldn't be overloaded. I always took that as an allusion to my corpulence. I was a bit exasperated, and I asked Tommy:

"And you, Tommy, how much do you weigh?"

"Two hundred and twelve pounds and six foot three in my work boots."

We were a hundred kilos over. I took the co-pilot's seat, and we waited on the tarmac more than an hour because of the thick fog that had descended on the camp. Sometimes it lasted for a week. I was surprised to see that Tommy had a hickey on his neck, shaped like Melville Island. How could that be? I'd left our room at four a.m. I'd seen no girl in his bed. I hoped that this mark on his skin hadn't come from Marcelline. Tommy seemed nervous as he sat beside me. He clearly had things to say.

Seeing my impatience, he began by giving me the details of the taxidermy business in which he and Rosaire had been involved. Besides being our pilot and knowing how to make excellent fishing lures, Tommy knew how to obtain official papers for sending a polar bear across the Atlantic - to Parisian collectors, for example, which was no small job.

"Your brother liked the bears a lot, you know. I'd asked him to find me some stuffed ones for Brice's European business."

"Hunters and their obsessions are hard to figure out, never mind deal with."

"He helped us to ship the payload in the refrigerated holds of ore tankers leaving the Arctic for Rotterdam. Hardly anyone in the crews knew about it. We moved the perishable foodstuffs into a cold storage space in the kitchen for as long as the ship was to be at sea."

"That sounds very dangerous. I'm surprised at my brother."

"But all of that was to make us very rich. The Golden Calf, Brice's former store, paid up to thirty thousand Euros for an adult polar bear if the fur was in good condition. Some liked to make carpets out of them with the animal's mouth closed, while others, like the Russians, kept the jaws wide open to show their menacing teeth."

"Money was never a priority for my brother," I said, unbelieving.

"The Russians, especially high-ranking politicians and oil magnates, love extreme taxidermy. I suspect they even arranged for the theft of a throne made of narwhal tusk from the Louvre to enrich a private collection. Narwhal tusks are very rare and in high demand, as you know. Narwhal ivory was even used in the Hapsburg sceptre."

"You know a whole lot about taxidermy! As for the theft from the Louvre, I heard about that throne on the news."

Tommy said nothing. He seemed not to be listening to me anymore, intent on lifting the plane into the air.

I'd thought Rosaire's interest in taxidermy was only that of an amateur, but what Tommy was telling me had nothing to do with a hobby. As we were flying over the snowy peaks, Tommy defended traditional hunting and took aim at the so-called environmentalists.

"Hunting for us is an ancient tradition, and 'green' tourism is a disaster. I hate all these young vegetarians with glasses, who insulate their houses with old jeans because asbestos is poisonous, and dream of building a cabin in the country out of recycled materials."

"You're kind of exaggerating, Tommy."

"I am not! The activists from all over the world who invade Churchill and take photos of the polar bears do them more harm than the hunters. The only reason the bears come down to Churchill is because the town is so full of tourists and they know they'll find stuff to eat."

"I think there've always been bears in Churchill in the spring."

"No, Ambroise, not as many. Before, people who lived there were afraid of those wild animals and chased them away with their pick-ups. Today, the bears rule the local economy. The tourist invasion is encouraged, with amateur photographers and film crews that entice the bears with jars of pickled herring, cans of sardines, or barrels full of jam busters."

"Yes, Churchill is like a dangerous wild zoo."

"Those friends of Greenpeace don't understand that with their 'innocent' activities, they're doing more harm to the animal than the Inuit hunt, because they're changing the bears' behaviour. In the end, they're putting them in danger and there's no cure for that. They're destroying their instincts. At the town dump, a bear died after trying to swallow a car battery. Another devoured a female jogger."

"It's true, I heard that in the spring they sometimes close schools because of the bears roaming around."

I said that to calm him, knowing perfectly well that the relations between the Inuit and environmental groups were not good.

Taxidermy was not a common art in Paris, but the curious shop on the rue de la Monnaie, bought by Brice de Saxe Majolique, and founded by Jean-Baptiste Deyrolle in 1831, was its Mecca. This man was a renowned entomologist, whose son, Achille, became famous for having stuffed a Sri Lankan elephant. The Golden Calf was a curio cabinet. You could find there lunar maps as well as stuffed zebras. Elephant feet were used for low tables or for stools. According to Tommy, Rosaire had helped Brice de Saxe Majolique put together his stock of narwhal tusks and what would become polar bear carpets. I had the sudden impression that one of those non-existent mountain ranges was rising up before me. This story seemed to me to be as big as a Fata Morgana mirage. Did Tommy know my brother better than I did?

25

The Golden Calf

Brice de Saxe Majolique understood very early on that even if you've inherited great genes, you don't necessarily have a gift for inner happiness. Happiness is a choice you make, a way of being you have to cultivate over time. Sometimes fate decrees that you must commit yourself to it with increasing passion in order to combat your destructive instincts. It's easier to become a drug addict than to run a marathon. It's easier to indulge in all your vices than it is to eat tofu four times a week. It's easier to make a thousand excuses for yourself than to run through the snow wearing snowshoes. And so he decided to work, though it made him unbearable to everyone else in his family.

His first plan was to rent out rooms to tourists, in his Seventh Arrondissement palace. The Lavirotte Building was an art nouveau curiosity, smack in the middle of a reserved, neo-classical neighbourhood. It was adorned with stone vines and marble artichokes, while its wrought iron gate and its windows reminded one of a giant fly's head over which Adam and Eve presided after the Fall. Black onyx butterflies with delicate wings darkened the façade. In the entryway, one was greeted by the bust of a woman draped in a fox boa. A dwelling with excessive flourishes designed to trump aristocratic ennui. But Brice de Saxe Majolique had taken up with the Italian maid he'd hired. She lived in a nine metre square room under the roof, and the herbs she grew on her little balcony fascinated him. Brice loved to sit there for hours on end. He drank dolcetto d'Alba, an Italian red wine that was almost black. He didn't want to go back down to his vast apartment with its crushed marble floors. He preferred the simplicity of his maid's room. He liked to listen over and over to a raspy recording of throat-singers, which inspired in him the idea that each of us must learn to live simply, to divest one's self each day of one object or one preconceived idea. He had even begun to bring tomatoes Provençal to the homeless person who stationed himself on Sunday mornings at the corner of avenue Rapp, until the man let him know that he favoured stuffed tomatoes. We are often disappointed by the reactions of others and even Brice de Saxe Majolique was not immune. Gold serves as an enhancement to powerful men, but it can never cure their existential malaise: it only makes it worse.

By renting his apartment, the taxidermist prince wanted to offer tourists what they dreamed of. To give them a taste of life. But his contacts with these people, some of them quite vulgar, weren't easy. Many were ignorant, constantly asking the same questions, treating him like a concierge. He had to carry their bags. If he was so rash as to leave a jar of sour cherry jam in the refrigerator, his loutish guests felt free to slather it on their bread. They had no refinement, but conducted themselves like ill-bred tenants. The whole business consumed all his time and energy, and distanced him from his deep, still unspoken desire to seek out new lands.

It was the oil portrait on wood of one of his ancestors with a degree in philosophy that compelled him to look for work. One spring morning, seated beneath the portrait's gaze, he realized that Paris could easily live without him and he found that depressing. He was searching for who he was. He'd taken courses in fencing, in navigation, in Italian cuisine, but nothing eased his existential gloom. He seemed to have been born with no vocation and this void would haunt him all his life. It was a function of his not really knowing himself. He simply did not understand what he wanted. One of his first romantic ideas had been to sell edible flowers at the Rungis market. But our prince in crisis could not see himself operating in such a plebeian environment. Brice de Saxe Majolique finally opted for business and taxidermy.

In a small plane flying over the glacial dome, Tommy explained how

Brice de Saxe Majolique and my brother did business together. Tommy assured me that Brice refused requests that were too exotic, such as a dress made from partridge bills for Jean-Paul Gaultier. You had to respect the animal's dignity. Though if you trust the archives, Salvador Dali allegedly obtained rhinoceros tusks at the Golden Calf. A devastating fire destroyed the business in 2007, and all was lost except for two small green parakeets. To finance reconstruction of the building, Hermès produced a limited edition silk scarf, embroidered with a Canadian polar bear. Illegal operations proliferated after the fire too, to get the bankrupt company back on its feet. Another goal of the trafficking was to compromise high-ranking Russian government officials with a view to tarnishing their reputations and bringing to light their true intentions in the Arctic. A complicated affair with many ramifications. Tommy implied that Brice de Saxe Majolique was a businessman with no conscience where the Golden Calf was concerned. He was prepared to do anything to defend the business.

The sky had gone black. There was a storm nearby. In the little cabin, dark now, I was losing my bearings. I realized that Brice might have killed my brother. Lightning was sure to strike the plane and send us to the bottom of a lake.

26

The Ice Pilot

In the Arctic Archipelago, there are so many lakes that people have never had time to name them all. We were flying over one of those remote expanses under hostile weather conditions, far from the inhabited land masses.

A severe blizzard was blowing. The cabin shook. Tommy told me that the weather was too bad to land near Iqaluit. We had to make a sudden shift towards the north. He suggested we land on Lake Mingo, before heading back down to Iqaluit. We had to wait for better conditions. The plane's windshield was fogged up, and Tommy had to rub it with his sleeve to see the frozen surface of the lake. I became more and more anxious, certain that we were done for. The plane seemed to be bouncing off the clouds. Now that I understood how close Tommy was to Rosaire, I saw him differently. Could I depend on him? My life was in his hands. The turbulence was extreme, and one of the blades on the right propeller cracked on landing. I also wondered whether the thin ice at this time of year might not give way under the weight of the plane. As usual, Tommy stayed calm. Before we left Kimmirut, I'd seen him trim the brush plane's blades with a saw to get more of a thrust on takeoff. I thought vaguely of my mother, and pulled myself together.

Tommy knew this lake well and tried to reassure me. This was the best thing for us to do. He had fixed up a hunting camp on the shore of Lake Mingo, which he called, affectionately, "Moccasin Camp." He had paid ten thousand dollars for it as part of the Canadian government's Arctic settlement program and he hoped to retire there one day. That was where we were going to seek shelter.

"The first time I came here, it was the smell of dampness and linseed oil that hit me right away. The door had been shut for decades. Inside the cabin, all the walls were covered with a strange green moss. I spent a month cleaning the wood with a brush I found in the high grass near the shore. Then I rubbed the walls with vinegar and replaced all the broken window panes."

Tommy had just put a kettle on the fire with water and threw in some blackberry leaves. Soon scented steam rose up, releasing their ferrous essence into the air.

"I see you're good with your hands! You did a great job."

"The hardest thing was the roof. It's made of tree trunks. I had trouble getting it even."

"We're pretty well set up here," I replied politely.

"I fixed up the old furniture, too. The table with the rounded corners, I sanded it down by hand. I painted the dresser white. It's here that I felt I was building something for the first time," Tommy said, moved.

From the windows you could see the lake slipping into its hidden beaches. Everything was unbelievably calm. No one knew about this camp except his eighty-eight-year-old great-aunt, who loved beaver soup, and who came here alone in the summer to hunt. Suddenly I was scared. Why had Tommy taken this huge detour? Why had we stopped at his hunting camp? Why all these confidences? Was Tommy going to kill me?

"You know, Ambroise, if I had studied I might have become a glaciologist, like Marcelline. Glaciology is a white man's invention..."

"Right," I agreed, as calmly as possible.

"When I was very young, one year at the beginning of July, in a big field of wild blueberries, I found a little family of white foxes that I was able to catch and put into a big cage. Six little foxes hung on their mother's teats, while the father tried to gobble fruit through the bars. At night they were very noisy. From the cage there came abdominal grunting, cries from deep down. It chilled the blood. My father got up one night and killed them all with his knife. He said that the foxes, even if I'd let them go, wouldn't have survived. It was a July with two full moons. My father made boots out of the male's skin, and used the little ones' fur to decorate them. After that I never saw life the same way again."

Tommy seemed lost in his memories. He admitted nervously that he found it hard to imagine his future. He didn't think he had any particular mission on this earth. When he was small, he dreamed of following in the steps of the scientists who arrived by plane: walking through blue caverns, cutting out ice cores and placing them in his knapsack, taking samples from rivers formed from melting icebergs and sending them to the Arctic Research Institute. But after he got his pilot's license, he had to say goodbye to his childhood dream. He felt useful ferrying people between the Iqaluit airport and the Kimmirut camp. The community had so much need for him.

27

The Strait of Anian

Held back in the hunting camp with Tommy, I saw my life pass before my eyes along with that of my ancestors. Jean Nicolet's worst mistakes could be attributed to his fears. To calm myself, I took my brother's notebook out of my bag. Intrigued and curious, I was looking for answers in its pages. I read a few, before I told Tommy the story.

In 1618, Jean Nicolet heard that you could reach China by way of the Bonne-Espérance headland. The Antarctic seas were violent though, and rife with wily sirens. He thought he might find a secret passage to the west thanks to Admiral Zheng He's Chinese map. At the far end of the inlet he had drawn, leading to the west and its inland seas, lay the mysterious Strait of Anian, the promised route to China and Japan.

During the long sea voyage that led him to New France, Jean Nicolet hid the rolled-up Chinese mappemonde in a wooden pietà with peeling paint that he had nailed onto the ship's prow to protect it. Nicolet wanted above all to be a good servant to the king. He had been chosen as a translator to live with the Allumette Island Indians and learn their language. He already saw himself as a great diplomat, bringing the native people and France closer together.

Nicolet set out with ten men he considered trustworthy. Sailors who told good stories. People with a generous nature. Men of action, who would help him achieve his goal: to find a passage to China. Hope is a rare thing. Hope, as Galileo knew, is a feeling of certainty married to a point of view. Few men bear within themselves the visionary intuition that makes everything possible. The cook was one of those men: he had already travelled on a frigate as far as Japan and had come back with an intense love for that country's beef, which he often talked about. He claimed that Kobe beef was as tender as butter and had a texture veined like cipolin marble, because the fat ran through the inside of the muscles, and not around them. This cook knew how to make the crossing pleasant by recounting his memories. One night, he told them how in Japan, after eating some strange dried mushrooms, he found himself unable to breathe. His larynx swelled up. Faced with this allergic reaction, he thought he would die. Fortunately, a young Japanese woman who was a picture of beauty came to save him, applying hot compresses to his brow all night long.

One May day, while the ship was sailing with Europe at its back, a storm blew up. The lemon-yellow sun vanished behind a threatening cloud cover. Waves higher than cathedrals crashed down onto the ship's bridge. The pietà came loose from its base and rolled along the bridge as the ship rolled with the waves. Nicolet went pale. He didn't know whether he was going to lose his mappemonde.

I stopped reading. These pages had the power to calm my emotions and to bring me comfort.

28

A Rosewood Laguiole

I was trapped in Moccasin Camp with Tommy, and it was impossible for me to reach Mitsy, which enraged me. I kept thinking about my brother and who had killed him. I was in despair. You could say that I was on the brink of madness. I thought constantly about Rosaire's last days, and Tommy's revelations concerning my brother left me perplexed.

"Your brother was a strange one, right? He told me a weird story a little over two weeks ago, when we were hunting in the Meta Incognita Peninsula."

"Someone hard to pin down, yes. I'm finding that I knew very little about him."

"So listen... This happened in Montreal, during the first weeks he was seeing Lumi. One day Rosaire got home after eight o'clock, with a little package under his arm that he'd gone to pick up at the post office. He seemed happy. Lumi was resting, lying on the couch. Sitting at the kitchen table, Rosaire opened the package. He had ordered from France a rosewood Laguiole pocket knife. A very beautiful object. He showed it to me while he told me the story. He'd unfolded the knife's blade and made a gesture as if to stab someone. Then, without knowing how or why, he planted the knife in his thigh. The gouge went ten centimetres into his flesh. Then he pulled out the knife, scared and incredulous. Blood flowed down his leg and onto his sock. He was a bit drunk. Unable to react, he cried before he fainted: 'Lumi, I don't know what's happening to me.' When he came to, Lumi was looking down on him, her arms crossed. She seemed irritated."

"That's incredible. He never told me that story."

"Lumi didn't budge. Rosaire called himself a taxi to go to Sacré-Coeur Hospital. They gave him thirty-two stitches on his thigh, which left him with an impressive scar."

I felt betrayed by my brother's silence. Rosaire had shut me out of a good part of his life. If he had told me this story, I would most likely have admitted that I still blamed him for when he shot me in the buttocks. Telling him that might have brought us closer together.

29

The Calgary Arctic Institute

After these hours spent in close quarters with Tommy, I began to think that it might still be possible to seduce Marcelline. There was nothing exceptional about the man. The problem was more Marcelline's: she seemed uninterested in men. She often said that they asked for everything and offered very little in exchange. She didn't believe in Prince Charming and declared sarcastically that for a woman to want to be a man's equal meant she had to lower herself.

During our long late evening conversations in the cafeteria, Marcelline sometimes confided in me. She had spent her childhood reading books in which children were persecuted by adults before being abandoned on desert islands, surviving thanks to their sense of direction and a Swiss Army knife. She needed no one. Marcelline was also self-taught. She had learned to ski all by herself, from a book. She'd become a respected militant environmentalist and her work as a glaciologist was the result of brilliant scientific studies. Only a sharp eye could detect in her uncertain handwriting the fragile little girl from a bad neighbourhood.

She'd had a boyfriend, Chad, a soldier who spent most of his time with his army buddies. She could never tolerate them, as she couldn't stand their fights. She was even afraid to go home at night to Chad and his gang of backward soldiers. She was sure they were going to argue over the dishes, over her dream of going to work in Nunavut, over how to cook a steak. She tried everything: a tea made with conifer needles, prayers, spells. She even drank a mouthful of her own blood. All that remained was to head for the Far North. There, she knew that she would find peace. She often said that it was either that or carrying around a flask of vodka in her skirt pocket, like her mother.

Chad was puffed up with pride and a pre-Copernican ego: he thought that sun revolved around him. He was a heliocentric. He wore his military uniform to go to the grocery store, to visit his mother on Sunday or to have lunch at the corner restaurant. Marcelline saw the Arctic as her only way to break free from the black moods of this spoiled child. There, she would never let anyone do her harm.

When Marcelline left for Kimmirut, she brought along two things: a small pistol for a woman, and a fossilized nautilus. Alone, she felt glorious. She said that it was only in the presence of others that she felt imperfect.

The last night she spent with Chad, she prepared a ray fish in black butter, his favourite dish. He gobbled it up with carefree joy. The ray is a flat-bodied cartilaginous fish with triangular pectoral fins connected to the head. Marcelline felt as though she was glowing in the dark when she crept down the corridor at midnight with her suitcases. Finally she was going to get noticed thanks to her doctoral studies at the Calgary Polar Institute. But she soon realized that she didn't want to become a professor. Speaking to five people in a closed room with graphics on an overhead-projector didn't interest her. The Kimmirut camp was perfect for her. Field work was the cure for her university days. She analyzed and catalogued data on ice, detected variations and different colours. She measured the speed of icebergs adrift in the sea, analyzed ice jams and movements of the tides. One morning, the bay might be empty of ice. The next day, the fog lifted over a sea weighed down with icebergs that whitened the landscape. The day after, a trio of sun dogs shone in the sky.

In the mine, Marcelline learned to love the din of the drills and the jargon of the mine workers she heard in the cafeteria, even if she preferred the company of stones and minerals to men. The endless Arctic night of winter lent itself to meditation. At the North Pole nothing was white, all was black: the lava cliffs and the children's hair. And summer, when the sun set for only an hour, all was brown and arid like in the desert. The last thing she needed was the unpredictable love of an ice pilot.

30

The Resurrection of Jaïre's Daughter

My love for Marcelline helped me to endure the monotony of waiting at Moccasin Camp. She was the most elusive of women, but when I left that place I was going to do everything I could to be with her. Marcelline made my life worth living. For all sorts of reasons, I loved her. I loved her for the way she prepared delicious ice cream on Friday nights. Lost in the Arctic, she was able to come up with astonishing flavours. Her secret: a small jute bag that contained vials of essential oils. Sometimes at night I would get up, put on my boots, coat, balaclava, and brave the cold to go back to the kitchen. There, I opened the little plastic buckets that Marcelline kept in the refrigerator and I sampled her sorbets. Marcelline made enough to open a gelateria. And so I tasted all the flavours: *fleur de lait,* Sicilian pistachio, sea salt, rosemary, lavender, melon-absinthe, coriander-lime, yellow watermelon, pink grapefruit and basil. My favourite: carnation ice cream. If Marcelline had prepared it, I would have tried turpentine. You couldn't analyze her cuisine, you could only breathe it in, drink it up. She brought an exotic touch to our inflexible North.

After hours that seemed like days, we were finally able to take off from Moccasin Camp at the end of the evening. We went back to Kimmirut, because the storm was raging over Iqaluit. I had abandoned the idea of talking to Mitsy. However, my long talks with Tommy had given me the courage to kiss Marcelline that very night. Tommy might have been born in an igloo, but I was now persuaded that I was better suited to her.

On our arrival, Marcelline had just put her hair into a pony tail, held in place with a braid made into a ring. She wore an oversize apron, jeans and a T-shirt with an Inuktitut inscription on the back: "The road to nowhere." I had asked her the day before to help me finish the engagement cake for Brice and Marie-Perle. In my absence, she had taken matters into her own hands. The peach melba cake, at Marie-Perle's request, had six layers, and was decorated with lily of the valley made from homemade almond paste. It was as if Marcelline were preparing her own wedding cake. I went into my glassed-in office to check the orders and the accounts. I couldn't take my eyes off Marcelline, who no doubt felt my heavy gaze on the back of her neck. I tallied my inventory in the cold pantry, counting the cartons of fresh figs for the reception. I told myself that an entrée of figs and prosciutto would really clash. Marie-Perle had discovered it at a tapas tasting during a trip to Las Vegas with Brice. At least I'd be able to satisfy someone who ate more than apple turnovers and roast beef. It would cost an arm and a leg but she was the boss's fiancée. I was paid to please, whatever the cost. Some employees preferred to stay at the camp during their vacations because they were so well fed.

I was counting the remaining milk cartons, my pencil in my mouth, when Marcelline came into the cold pantry looking for a container of ripe blackberries. On tip toe, she tried to reach the top level of the fruit cart. It was then that I noticed the blond fuzz that covered her lower back, between her jeans and her slightly pulled-up sweater. Without thinking, I placed my hand on her back, where there were two small dimples. She turned towards me, a bit shaken. I brought my hand up under her sweater and placed it on her breast. I took Marcelline's face in my hands and looked at it, stunned, then I placed my lips on hers. Her body was warm. Our kiss generated an opaque mist. We made love against the crates of romaine. Our bodies bumped against the brittle wood, on which could be read: *Product of Salinas California*. At every thrust, she heaved a guttural sigh. Her legs were hooked around me and I was supporting her buttocks. She was light, she was spare. She seemed to purr. Her lips were going blue in the glacial air of the cold room. Our saliva would soon freeze. Her body and breasts tasted like a coffee cream puff, a pistachio macaroon, like vanilla ice cream. Later I slipped into the pocket of her apron a piece of butcher's paper on which I had written this sentence: "Marcelline, I would like to inhale your pistachio skin all night." At last she was mine.

When we emerged from our shelter, frozen, Marcelline's lips were purple. She quickly returned to her tent. I felt she was ashamed that she had succumbed, fearing the new dynamic that her act had created. In her tent she kept a painting reproduced by a village elder converted by one of the Mormons who roamed around Iqaluit. "The Resurrection of the Daughter of Jaïre," depicting a mortal's being brought back to life. Marcelline wanted to believe in God and she made the effort, visiting the mine's chapel every morning. At the little school, the religious order staged a crucifixion every Easter and every year she fell in love with whoever played Jesus. I was myself thrown off balance by what had just happened, as though I had at last been given my first chance in life.

31

The Secret

I went to join Marcelline in her tent to ask her if she needed to be consoled. I wanted to be with her, it was more than I could bear. The light outside was so strong that your eyelids gave little protection against the sun. She was sleeping, a scarf wound around her head. I lifted the cloth to wake her. She was in a bad mood and felt a little insulted by my using the word "consoled," but she soon relaxed, telling me why she sometimes seemed so cold. I settled down on the neighbouring bed, delighted and astonished to be admitted into this sacred chamber. She placed a perforated warming pan full of ashes over her bed to provide some heat. I was in a drugged state, having her near me.

She explained to me that she had lived under terrible conditions when she was very young. Her mother, who raised her children on her own, allowed them only one shower a month. Marcelline had to wash herself like a little cat. Most often she swam secretly in the river, in the midst of pike, sewage that had leaked from septic tanks, and lily pads. She became, out of necessity, a warrior, a recruit engaged in an obscure struggle. Marcelline had suffered indescribable abuse from a neighbour, who was also an occasional lover of her mother. At night, he used a ladder to climb onto the roof of the prefabricated house, and entered her room, the only one on that floor, through the window. He made love to her on her bed and its pink quilt decorated with little pompoms. He took her from behind, one hand over her mouth, the other on her flat belly. He drooled into her black hair. But he couldn't spend much time watching his sex pumping in and out, as he had trouble prolonging his pleasure. He wasn't interested in her breasts, which were two little teats that he eyed only at the beach, when her mother let her swim in a monokini. He liked to feel himself wedged inside her. Over the years, she got used to her aggressor. He was the only man she knew. Those nightly encounters became their secret. The first time, she was thirteen. She thought that one day he would take her with him, far away.

One night, alerted by the strange noises from upstairs, her mother quietly entered the bedroom. By the light of the little pink lamp she saw the neighbour totally naked, lying on his side, his arm bent, his head resting in one hand while the other caressed Marcelline's round buttocks through her Fraisinette nightie, as she read a book. Her mother went to get a cast iron frying pan from the kitchen, and knocked him cold while he was trying to do up his jeans. Marcelline cried out. Her mother shattered the man's skull, almost killing him. She was sentenced to eighteen months in prison for unpremeditated attempted murder.

In my room I had a book called *Blood: Ten Ways to Prepare It*. Listening to Marcelline as she confided in me, I imagined the full meal I could cook up with her neighbour's blood. A Neapolitan *sanguinaccio,* or *crème brulée* with blood. A *sangre frita,* a very common dish in Europe during the Middle Ages. An Estonian blood bread, Florentine blood crêpes, apple blood sausage. Marcelline went silent. To break the quiet, I listed all the dishes I was keeping in reserve for her aggressor. She burst into liberating laughter. If I'd had this man before me, I would have impaled him with the warming pan.

Sunday morning, I woke up alone in Marcelline's tent. I rushed to my phone, and finally succeeded in reaching Mitsy at the Iqaluit radio station. She told me that she'd lost the cell phone I'd been trying to contact her on since the day before. I informed her that the sentence written on the base of the pietà recovered in Iqaluit was the same as the one scrawled on the forearm of my brother before his death. She didn't know that, and would follow the trail. I trusted her more than the police, who, at last word, were much more interested in a stuffed polar bear head in the Arctic Circle bar. The famous animal, stuffed sixty years earlier, had been moulded from a ton of newspapers, and now the fire department was being brought in. Since the blaze in the Iqaluit church, people were more afraid of fire than of death.

32

Heave ho!

Marie-Perle's favourite expression was: "It's impossible." She had the perfect profile for a future housewife. At Brice's suggestion, she wore maternity pants every other day. She told the girls in the cafeteria that the elastic kept her tummy warm. Finally she was going to get married and once that was over and done there would be only one item left on the list: to make a baby. For her engagement, Marie-Perle had chosen a sleeveless jacket in fake beaver, and jeans so tight you'd have thought they'd been painted onto her legs.

To get along with Brice you just had to pretend that everything was his idea. I'd chosen background music for the engagement party, Donizetti's "The Daughter of the Regiment." When Brice passed through the kitchen in the morning, I said: "Good choice of music." He gestured with his hand, as if he were cutting his throat.

The worst was yet to come for him. Idleness bears no fruit but constant torment. Marie-Perle would soon start complaining to her husband that she didn't feel well. Brice told her that she had to eat for everything to get back to normal. She invented imaginary illnesses. Brice had certainly chosen to marry her because he needed some affection, but he was going to suffer for it. Sex with Marie-Perle was already mechanical and brusque. Almost professional. Marie-Perle was so cold, so thin. The time for sex, president to apprentice, was already over. He knew Marie-Perle too well to be able to make love to her without shutting his eyes.

The first day they met, he thought he was dealing with a free woman with great strength of character. As time went on, her weaknesses came to light, and she could no longer play a role for him. Rosaire had told me that sex was in large part imagination, with its shadowy zones, and always at its best with a stranger. From Brice, Marie-Perle demanded total submission. And environmentally correct jaunts to distant communities where she could shop for local crafts.

I went to Marcelline's greenhouse to see what miracle herbs she could provide me with. I found her laying down a mixture of guano, ground-up antlers, and dried blood, a natural fertilizer recommended for sterile ground.

"That's not very vegetarian, beef blood. Did you sleep all right? You're up so early," I said softly.

"You always want to keep track of what I'm doing. For the fertilizer, I have no choice, nothing else works," she replied, brusquely.

"You could ask for organic certification. It could work here, elsewhere it's always a lot trickier," I added, to defuse her anger.

"I don't understand."

"The problem is that your neighbour will never be organic. His copper insecticide spray is bound to reach your plants, either through the air or the water table."

"That's true," Marcelline answered, visibly cowed.

"Where's Marie-Perle? I haven't seen her this morning."

"She's sleeping," replied Marcelline, forming a pillow with her hands. "She's been anorexic since her teens and the condition has never gone away. She's too depressed to eat. She's running on ketones. It's common for women with eating disorders. Hunger followed by a burst of euphoria."

"I confess that I've never seen her eat anything more than an egg white omelette with mushrooms. She orders it every day. That dish must give you a hundred and sixty calories, max."

"And she wants me to grow at least one pot plant in my greenhouse. She used to inject herself with Botox in the mirror in the Arctic Circle's ladies' room."

"To tell the truth she looks a little like Brice's greyhound," I remarked, to make Marcelline smile.

Absorbed in Brice's life, Marie-Perle forgot her own. The people around her suffered the most from her bitterness. Without mastery over her own fate, she passively drifted through life and blamed others for it. She clung to the role of victim. My mother used to say: "Don't spend time with people who don't enjoy eating, they don't like life." The night of her engagement, Marie-Perle doubled her antidepressant prescription, ordered through an Internet pharmacy in China that sent her medicine labelled as flowers. The name Siam Florist appeared on her bank statements,. All her life she had wanted to marry, but now she was sinking into a deep dark abyss, just when she thought she'd found perfect happiness.

We arranged little bouquets of poppies and Arctic roses on the tables. I wanted to serve fish stew for dinner, but it was impossible to please all the people working for NGOs, Environment Canada's vegetarians, Greenpeace's lacto-vegetarians, the pesco-vegetarians and ovo-vegetarians. All these people, defined by what they refused to put into their mouths, got on my nerves. The spiritual dimension of vegetarianism was something that always eluded me. This banquet required a lot of concentration. I would have preferred to raise my sails and head elsewhere, but the reception was very beautiful and turned out well. I was just happy that the alcohol ban was lifted for one night.

I sat down briefly at the fiancés' table. Kujjuk's father, a rich and important man in the region, recounted the myth of "the woman who does not want to marry." I learned that the heaviest burden for Inuit women was to ensure the reincarnation of those in their family who had passed on. A woman wearing a traditional red parka told of her birth, claiming that her genealogical memory went back to the fourteenth century. She added that for the reincarnation process to succeed you had to cut the umbilical cord with a stone, but never with an imported metal blade. She also described the ritual celebrations of *tivaajut,* which took place at the winter solstice, when everyone had to imitate the cry of the bird whose skin was used to sponge them off at birth.

Brice drank too much and started to talk about how Marie-Perle always had her eye on him. To avoid her outbursts, he had to rein himself

in. During their first trip to France, he hadn't told her he was transport-
ing vacuum-packed bear steaks in his baggage. It was illegal, and she
could have done anything to sabotage him, even turning him in to the
customs agent. He went on to describe her family from hell. It was only
midnight but for him it was already too late. Marie-Perle vomited in the
toilet, and I helped Brice back to his lodgings.

Now their pipe dream could truly begin. Marie-Perle would stay with
Brice to protect her life of leisure. She would undertake an ongoing cycle
of consumption, buying things she couldn't afford and didn't need, just
to impress the people she hated. This woman of the demimonde had
Brice in her net. She had hitched him to her life and was now towing him
towards her shores, the better to drown him.

Marie-Perle loved to denigrate others, too. Above all, she enjoyed
speaking badly of Lumi, even while giving her wide smiles whenever
they met. She had never forgiven her treason, and embarked on a long
and tenacious campaign designed to slander her.

The thin thread of trust is extremely fragile. Never place your fate in
someone else's hands, because there may always be something going on
behind the scenes. Too few people understand that when you harm a
neighbour, the act always rebounds in another form: a violent influenza,
infections, chicken pox with its scars, poisoned marriages. Or just the
taste of despair lodged at the bottom of the throat for all eternity. A metallic taste that not even alcohol can take away.

33

The Loyal Goose

The Inuit believe in reincarnation. They will tell you to never speak badly of your mother-in-law because she'll get even with you when she comes back to earth in the guise of your son. Tommy often starts his sentences with the words: "When I was my paternal grandfather..." He is convinced that he was his grandfather because since birth he has had a bit of a squint in his left eye, and his grandfather lost the same eye in a hunting accident.

Monday morning, feeling I had done my duty, I went to meet Brice to confirm that I could take my vacation in Montreal. On my way, an enormous flight of geese darkened the sky. Canada geese are very faithful animals. Inseparable, they live in couples all their lives. The birds are immense and their migration is spectacular, almost moving.

Approaching Brice's office, I was blocked by a tremendous backup of dump trucks along the road. In the middle of the road was an enormous grey and black female goose who was watching over the crushed remains of her partner. She was determined to stay with her late companion, prodding him with her beak now and then. The workers were getting impatient. The driver of the first truck in line got out of his vehicle, picked up the corpse of the large flattened goose and threw it to the edge of the road. Thwack! The female kept trying to revive her partner by nudging him with her beak. The traffic jam dissolved. The episode left me miserable.

Brice hadn't recovered from his emotions of the night before and seemed to be suffering from a serious migraine. He signed my vacation form while gulping down three aspirin. When I wanted to leave his office, he held me back by the wrist and, as though taking me into his confidence, said:

"Your brother was on a case that's important for the future of the country. He was trying to prove, along with a group of geologists, that the Lomonosov Ridge is connected to the Canadian continental shelf."

"Yes, I know."

"When the Russians planted their flag on the sea floor, the government reacted. Peter McKay, the Minister of Foreign Affairs, said 'This isn't the fifteenth century.'"

"Yes."

"Do you know that Chinese diplomats made demands to our government on the advice of Rosaire? They claim that the Arctic is international territory and that since the Chinese represent 22% of the world's population, they have the right to 22% of the Arctic's resources."

"That doesn't surprise me. They don't have their own resources. They have nothing, they have to buy everything. They flood villages to construct dams and produce electricity. They're desperate."

"Yes, strangely enough, the Chinese have even found an ancient map which could prove that they discovered America before Columbus. In 1418. The Canadian government, most of all the Inuit chiefs, hope the map will turn out to be a forgery. What's even stranger is that your brother seemed to know the details of this map very well."

"A number of copies exist, and one was part of our family history. Our ancestor had it when he travelled up the Saint Lawrence in search of China."

"That's impossible, Ambroise. Your ancestor? Then couldn't your brother have sold this map to the Chinese? Might Rosaire have betrayed his country? But why? The map is a forgery, isn't it?"

"I have no idea. It belonged to Admiral Zheng He, who was in the service of the third Ming Emperor. Like many of the Emperor's servants, he was a eunuch, and he carried his genitals around in a silver reliquary to ensure he'd be reincarnated as a whole man in his next life.

"At night he placed his reliquary at the base of a small lamp that served as an altar. In 1418, when the markets of Peking were full of thousands of books written by philosophers and encyclopaedists, Europe was still in darkness. Gutenberg hadn't developed his press and Henry V had only six books in his library."

"Indeed," Brice agreed, astonished at my knowledge.

"Zheng He's flotilla, known as the Armada of Treasures, was a vast, floating, commercial centre. Its holds contained the famous blue porcelain, Komodo dragon saliva and little jade cabbages – lucky charms that ensured food would always be abundant. Pepper served as currency for trade and sailors were intellectuals who sometimes knew more than ten languages. It's said that on board they sacrificed half their ration of water to grow fragrant rosebushes."

"Where did you learn all that?" asked Brice.

"Zheng He's map is part of our family heritage. On its back there is a strange inscription. Using a piece of raw indigo, someone traced the gold road leading to an incredible store of minerals. Zheng He must have visited what we now call the Canadian Arctic Archipelago."

"That's impossible," replied Brice.

Irritated, I simply turned on my heels and left his office for the last time.

34

A Japanese Man on the Ice Field

It was time I got to Montreal to plan Rosaire's funeral. Tommy played Dolly Partons's "Jolene" during the entire flight between Iqaluit and Montreal. On board the Sundog airplane, there was a Japanese science tourist. Tommy suddenly shouted, as we were flying over an ice desert above Baffin Island, "Is this where you want us to leave you?" The Japanese man checked his GPS and nodded. We stopped on an iceberg several kilometres long to let him off. Fortunately, he was accompanied by a polar bear handler, a little moon-faced Inuit. When we landed, the plane slid along a long sheet of milky ice strewn with star-shaped crystals, and a tire burst before Tommy brought the plane into a hairpin turn. He was a superb pilot: he'd apprenticed with Bearskin Airlines. Turning around, he looked at the Japanese tourist before remarking:

"If you get lost, do what Ross did when he was looking for Franklin: hang messages around the necks of snow foxes. They go back to camp to eat our garbage. If you're out of food you can also boil up your belt if it's made of leather."

Tommy changed the tire as if it was for a Chevy and we took off again.

After we lifted off, I kept my eyes on the Japanese researcher. Because of climate change, polar bears were hunting on tiny, drifting pack ice. They'd become particularly dangerous. I admired the man's courage. He mustn't have had a family, to embark on such an adventure.

Everyone at the mine wanted to go south for Rosaire's funeral, but I was able to discourage some of them. You couldn't just let things go up there. Wild animals would move into the camp. Just before I left, a bear that was a bit too curious had done damage to a helicopter where a pilot had left a bag of candy. Rosaire would have loved to witness that strange scene. Marcelline was set to join me in Montreal on Tuesday morning, the day before the burial.

As soon as I arrived, I went to my apartment. I was anxious to see what Rosaire had sent me. A padded envelope had been slipped through the slot in my door and lay on the floor among community newspapers and a flyer from World Vision, a humanitarian organization that sought donations for African countries.

On the envelope I made out some shaky handwriting that didn't look like my brother's:

My dear brother,

This envelope contains a letter to be read only if something happens to me. Don't ask any questions and mention it to me if everything's all right.

I opened the envelope at once.

Ambroise,

This is a strange situation... If you are reading this letter, it's because I am dead. I now know secrets I cannot reveal. But I can still tell you that I love you and that our fraternal relationship has been wonderful despite our little wars. I confess today that I regret that incident with the shotgun... You ought to have that lousy shot removed from your backside! Thanks to you, on this earth I had someone I could count on. I knew I could ask you for anything and you'd have done it without question. No one is really at ease on this planet. You have to be honest to admit it. We're all afraid. What's important is to find appropriate ways to combat fear. My mistake was in using women. They were my equilibrium and my downfall. I love you, and I'm giving you one last piece of big-brotherly advice. Live your life more simply than I lived mine. I had too many women and too many shady business deals. Find your way and your happiness and try to live an extraordinary life. Everything you need, you already possess. Because we are nothing without our history. When everything is lost, it's all that remains. In this dark North, we have already lived a thousand lives.

Now I must come to difficult matters. I believe that Lumi has killed me. I've discovered things recently that lead me to believe that she doesn't really love me. Lumi killed me for the money she would receive after my death. But she is no longer the beneficiary of the Sun Life policy I took out in her name this spring. If anything at all happens to me, single her out, her accomplices too. This message is my will. Do not leave Lumi free.

Your brother Rosaire, who values you greatly.

I didn't know what to think. With a pen, I mechanically filled out the World Vision form, making a donation. For a hundred dollars I had the choice of paying for medicine to cure a hundred children of diphtheria, buying school supplies for fifty, or stocking a stable in a Mauritanian village. I ticked off the square "stable: three chickens, a rooster, two goats and a cow," and I made the gift in Marcelline's name.

Reading the letter, I was beside myself. I was too fragile or emotional to be able to deal with such revelations. I dreamed of a simple, quiet life, but everything always seemed to turn poisonous. I felt dispossessed of my brother. Of everything.

35

The Inventory

Are we what we possess or what we build? That's the question I was asking myself on my way to Rosaire's and while I rummaged through his office. In this apartment he never went to, I felt like a thief. In a drawer I came across a loose piece of paper on which was transcribed the inventory of our ancestor's possessions. Jean Nicolet died on an October night in 1642, when he went out in a rowboat with M. de Chavigny to intervene in a war that pitted the Algonquin against the Iroquois. A young Iroquois had been taken hostage, his feet pierced with sticks of wood, his nails and teeth wrenched out. The day he was to be burned at the stake had been decided. Nicolet, a translator and friend to the Indians, was the only person who had a chance of reconciling the two tribes. A storm blew up, with high waves on the Saint Lawrence. Hanging on to the boat, which had overturned in the icy water, Jean Nicolet said to M. de Chavigny: "Sir, you know how to swim, I do not. I am going to meet God. I commend to you my wife and my daughter."

A few days after Jean Nicolet's death, an inventory was made of his belongings. Mention was made of a bed, a few wooden chairs, hunting and fishing equipment and leather chests and trunks adorned with studs and equipped with locks. His clothing was in the style of his best friend Champlain: black Morocco leather shoes, breeches made of serge from Frécamp, a Berry wool blouse with buttons, a scarlet bonnet, and a beaver hat with a silver cord and a white feather. Also found were a small cask of scents, two pipes of red stone with a box of tobacco in enamelled copper and a barber's kit with eight razors, four combs and two moustache-lifters. This list, reproduced in Jesuit Relations, had been photocopied by Rosaire. My brother had talked to me about it. It showed that our ancestor Nicolet smoked a lot, but the famous pietà that Rosaire had discovered the year before had not been catalogued.

Also at the bottom of the sheet were the books Nicolet owned: *The Inventory of Sciences, The Discoveries of the Portuguese in the Occidental Indies;* a collection *of Gazettes* from 1634; *The Art of Navigation; Gazettes* from 1635; *a* fencing manual; Ovid's *Metamorphoses; Relations from New France* from 1637; *the Tableau des Passions Vivantes; The Life of Saint Ursule; Meditations on the Life of Jesus Christ; Le Secrétaire de Cour; L'Horloge de Dévotion;* the address *To Live According to God; The Elements of Logic; The Holy Duties of the Pious Life; The History of Portugal;* a small satin-covered missal called *The Ritual of the Mass; The Life of the Saviour of the World;* two music librettos; *The History of the Occidental Indies;* a folio *Lives of the Saints;* and five other books whose titles were not identified.

In addition to this library there was a telescope, clock, four images representing the seasons in nature, four maps, and a painting of the Virgin.

In a curious way, reading this list consoled me. I who seemed never able to stay in one place since my brother's death, fell asleep on his bed for several hours before waking with a start: I had to contact the Iqaluit police to inform them of my brother's last wishes.

I thought about him all the following night. Rosaire was fortunate: he had pursued a career in international law, the most beautiful women threw themselves at his feet, and he still found reasons to complain. In truth, since the day he pulled that shotgun trigger, the latent tension between us had never gone away. I admit that I was jealous of him. He was a man who could elicit both love and hate. A man whom I often fled, that I now missed.

Since Rosaire's death, I'd been overcome by sadness that was dark and unresolved, cavernous. Rosaire would be buried in less than two days. That night I ordered flowers for the ceremony on interflora.ca, and for the sympathy message I chose this Buffon quotation from the scroll-down menu: "Most men die of sorrow."

36

We Drank Too Much Ice Wine

On Tuesday May 11, I was walking along the Lachine Canal, now transformed into a large well-groomed park. Under the graffiti-covered bridges where heroine addicts slept among the urban stables, the grain silos and the small workers' houses, I felt betrayed. Through the sun's rays I saw Marcelline coming towards me, and I thought I heard lightning crackle in the summer sky. When our hearts came closer, it was as if two tectonic plates were colliding head-on along the Saint Lawrence fault. Erasing the blue sky. Levelling the landscape with an industrial deluge. Her arms were full of yellow tulips, and she was pulling a red shopping cart with rubber wheels. She'd come from the market. It was the first time I'd seen Marcelline not bundled up in an Inuit coat, in Nunavut. She wore a plum-coloured silk sundress and a long necklace of dried beluga bones. We embraced and then we sat down across from the Silophone on the Quai Saint-Pierre to drink a good slug from the bottle of ice cider she had pulled out of her shopping bag. It was a yellow wine made from frozen apples, picked from their trees in the middle of winter. She said:

"You'd think it was a liquid version of those Moroccan pastries with honey and almonds. What do you think?"

"Honey on a buttered slice of bread."

She would come with me the next day to my brother's funeral. I said, as if my grief allowed me this audacity:

"Maybe if we had children together, we wouldn't have time to think about being so unhappy. When your hair's full of baby cereal, there are no more questions."

"You have to choose to be happy, Ambroise. Children don't stand in the way of unhappiness, depression, solitude or abandonment."

"That's true," I said. "My brother explained to me the Chinese idea of *Qi*, an organism's vital force. When a human being comes into the world, he possesses a certain genetic or karmic potential, but the individual must optimize this potential to have a long and happy life."

Marcelline took her time before replying:

"Once, an enologist from California explained that for a European, the most important factor is the wine's origins. If a Saint Emilion is good, it's because it comes from a rich region. The *terroir* creates a reaction that is almost cerebral. In Europe, you have to know where you come from and where you stand in the hierarchy. In our egalitarian New World, our origins aren't so important. It's what you are today that gives you value. We live in a meritocracy. New World wines are wines of effort, not of *terroir*. It's exactly the same for happiness."

Marcelline always changed the subject when we talked about children, or she went from pillar to post. The question scared her. She added in conclusion:

"We often make children to solve a problem that will stay unresolved."

When I talked with her, I sometimes felt as if I were participating in a scientific debate. But that pleased me. I took to hiding a carefully annotated journal like *Foreign Affairs* in the kitchen pantry . During our debates, I would refer to it. What we were seeking was the formula for happiness, and I was convinced that she would find it with my help. I wanted to sacrifice myself for her. It was then that I asked:

"And if you met your Prince Charming?"

"I hate Prince Charmings. In theory, Prince Charming has tons of gold stored away, and that gives him the right to impose the cooking, the dishes, the washing, and lovemaking twice a day requiring you to give a good loud cry and confirm his virility. In time you are granted the privilege of giving birth to his offspring, which adds twenty pounds to your weight and shuts you up in the palace for twenty years. That's enough for you to start abusing prescription drugs or psychotropic substances."

"That's a bit much, Marcelline."

"If I have hold of the purse strings, then I'll be free. I won't have to clean the bathtub. I'll ask men to do it instead. And they'll be happy to oblige. I'm lucky. My way has been paved by women who set fire to their Wonderbras fifty years ago. I'm not turning back the clock!"

"That really makes me want to be your husband. You want an exchange of servitude?"

"When I was born, I didn't have to ask myself: am I a woman or a man? Will being a woman cause me problems in the future? Those questions never came to mind. Listen, my mother worked all her life. She left in the morning, when Orion was still twinkling in the sky. When she gave birth, she went back to work three weeks later, otherwise there would have been nothing to eat. My brothers and I were never allowed the luxury of throwing tantrums. She didn't want to make us the centre of her universe. That's why I am the way I am. When you're a mezzo soprano, you don't end up with the prince, you are the prince."

Marcelline said all that with a great deal of pride, but I couldn't resist interrupting:

"But you have your own come-ons. The prehistoric Inuit tattoos on your arm are there to seduce us men, and it works, it works very very well. And the black nail polish, that's not there to attract us?"

The sweet wine was beginning to go to my head.

"No. It's just proof that I'm a well-behaved girl who always wanted to be a rebel, and never succeeded in doing so. The black nail polish is a beauty product with its own history. It's both non-conformist and aristocratic. It existed in ancient China, where the colour black was reserved for queens, and a punk boutique in London revived it in 1967. Later, Freddie Mercury began to wear it, but only on one hand, then David Bowie followed, along with other androgynous rock stars like Marilyn Manson. In 2003, even David Beckham, the soccer player, was photographed by *L'uomo Vogue* with his nails lacquered black."

We'd drunk too much ice cider, and our conversation was wandering from one subject to another, but it flowed like the first conversations of lovers, those that you no longer have after a few years of being together. I said, in a tone that tried to be reassuring:

"You have an answer for everything, and it's that attitude that's scary.

You should live from day to day. Relax. Not think too much..."

"That's very bourgeois, to live from day to day. If mothers who raise their children alone couldn't work, to fix all the meals, the kids would not survive. They do not live from day to day, they're always looking to the future."

"As I see it, you would be the S, and I would be the M. And we'd live happily to the end of our days. You'd put out my eyes with an ice pick, because according to you, I want to stay blind to other women."

"You know why the Inuit find that the white man smells of milk?" Marcelline was again trying to elude me.

"Marcelline, do you like Tommy? I saw him kissing you behind Violet Rock last winter. Because it was so cold, your breath rose six metres over your heads. It was impressive."

"I don't love Tommy. It's the cold that got to me that night, and I regretted it afterwards. You know he wasn't born in an igloo? He told me he'd invented that story to please the Whites. We all know how things work up there, no? On the flight back, everything was forgotten."

"That's all I wanted to know."

A surge of happiness filled my body. I smiled.

That night, the last before Rosaire's funeral, I realized that Marcelline had known the deep meaning of the word "unhappiness," and that she had chosen not to be her own executioner. It suddenly seemed clear to me that melancholy could only touch those who had never been prey to true unhappiness. The spring air calmed me, and in the shadow of Silo Number 5 our words repeated themselves, echoed. After the ice cider we drank white wine, a seyval from the Côtes-d'Ardoise, a Dunham vineyard. I will remember all my life what she said about it: "This wine is almost salty, it's as if one were breathing the Baffin sea air near the Kimmirut coast." Marcelline could see an ocean in a flask of wine.

I was astonished, following her to her apartment, to find so many windows and so little furniture. She said she did not accept gifts from friends, because every object weighed down her life. To console me, she cooked me aiguillettes of seitan, tasting of blood, with a red elderberry sauce. She had brought with her some sea urchins from Pond Inlet, and some Arctic salsify. There was something hard to grasp in Marcelline, a truth that alarmed me and a mystery that fascinated. She spoke little, but her words were unsparing. I never knew what she would do next.

That night she kissed me again and went to sleep drunk, repeating: "Ambroise, respect yourself. Respect yourself, Ambroise."

37

The Sailors' Chapel

Notre-Dame-de-Bon-Secours, the sailors' chapel, was filled with sunlight on this morning of Wednesday, May 12. The chapel, a building dating from 1771, was visited by anxious seamen preparing for the great Atlantic crossing. Looking at the little boats hanging as ex-votos from the vaulted ceiling, I thought of the pellet that I had in my behind, an eternal relic, within me, of my brother.

Brice de Saxe Majolique wore Oakley sunglasses with mirrored lenses that were far too wide. He had parked his goldfish-coloured Mustang convertible on a slope, below the church. He was certainly going to take advantage of the reception after the ceremony to persuade a dozen people to buy shares in the mine, arguing that the price was still low, and urging others to register for the conference, "Invest in the Market: A Special Mines and Metals Edition." The man clearly had no filter between his brain and his mouth. What he said to others served always as praise for himself.

Financial responsibility based on confidence is a concept peculiar to our economy. We're not used to having debts of honour. Rosaire owned a thousand shares in the mine at three dollars each. I always passed my turn when he suggested I buy some.

The priest was dressed in purple. I couldn't believe that I was attending my brother's funeral. From the beginning, I'd hoped that this whole story was just a joke, and that Rosaire would reappear. I kept repeating to myself something he had written me: "Don't be afraid that life is going to end. Be afraid that it will never begin." But I never wanted to make my life an exercise in personal growth.

Marcelline wore a black dress and a necklace of fresh water pearls that we fished on Sunday afternoons, in the autumn, at Kimmirut. In the vicar's office, thirty minutes before the ceremony, she had taken my hand and slipped into it a card with the holy image of Saint Lucie, patron saint of the blind. The saint was represented by eyeballs on a silver platter. Blinded because she tried to protect her chastity, she could always see, even after having lost her eyes. On the back of the image was a prayer for perfect vision.

I held the pious image up to my heart, before climbing to the pulpit to nervously deliver a tribute to my brother. All eyes were turned towards me, even those of Lumi, who was wearing Rosaire's stupid skunk hat. She was flanked by two policemen. She fixed me with a dark and frigid gaze. She no doubt thought I suspected her of having poisoned Rosaire with the container of antifreeze found in her pickup. I was very moved. In a trembling voice, I read what I had written on a sheet of paper that very morning:

One winter night in the pinewoods, when the sea-blue sky lined with trees sparkled with shooting stars, my mother wanted to show me the Great Bear by pointing to it with her finger. She told me how she had placed tiny little Rosaire in a snowbank, wrapped up in a one-piece snowsuit with an Eskimo hood. He was gazing at the starry vault when a meteorite passed across the sky. It was at that exact moment that my mother knew that Rosaire was going to have an exceptional destiny. According to her, he was blessed by the gods. Despite her best efforts, I was never able, that night, to make out the Great Bear, which I still, by the way, cannot identify. But I understood right then that Rosaire was different from other people, and from me. He was headstrong in his work and in his daily life. What he did for the Inuit of Nunavut was admirable. But today, under these sad circumstances, I want to remember the minute details of our relationship more than the great exploits of his life. A few weeks before he died, I was running at his side along Kimmirut's rocky beaches, our feet pounding the shiny algae on the pebbly trails bordered by blue rivers. Our heartbeats

were like instruments setting the pace for a great zest for life. Our steps, in har-
mony, resonated on the frozen ground. At one point Rosaire began to whistle,
and I felt his happiness. That was the last time I ran with him. And that's what
I feel I will miss the most.

I cleared my throat and returned to my seat in the first row, beside Marcelline. Lumi was sitting far behind me. I heard her sob, as if she had
been hired as a mourner. I felt bad. I could not continue to live among
all these liars. Who had killed Rosaire? Lumi, Brice? Who? I came very
close to standing up and causing a scandal.

During the reception that followed the ceremony, Brice told my parents about his last trip to Mexico. I see them still, upright, erect, facing
the Goldpan Prince. He asserted that developing countries are not as
disagreeable as is often believed. That the women are just as beautiful
as elsewhere, the golf clubs as luxurious and the distribution of wealth
comparable to that of Canada. After a few polite smiles, Marcelline and
I decided to go and eat in Chinatown, at Miss Hong Kong, Rosaire's favourite restaurant. Before leaving, still a bit drunk from the night before,
I said to Lumi:

"We'll be in Chinatown at Miss Hong Kong until four in the morning.
We'll be hanging out there all week, if you want to contact us."

I don't know where this all came from, but I said it. It must have been
dictated to me by my thinly veiled anger.

38

S&M

The day after Rosaire's funeral, I woke up with all my clothes on. On my night table there was a matchbook with the drawing of a golden limousine, and the logo of Miss Hong Kong. These vague words were scrawled on it: "Ambroise to pay." Had I left the restaurant without paying? Had we stayed at Miss Hong Kong all night? Before my mirror, I was short of breath. I was alone, with no Marcelline and no memory.

When there was a cave-in at the mine and some miners went missing, one always hoped that there was an air pocket in the shaft that would enable them to survive. At the mine entrance, a sign displayed the number of days without an accident. For forty-five days, nothing had happened.

An Iqaluit police officer phoned me in the morning to ask if the young glaciologist Marcelline Golden had had a relationship with my brother. He had just found the following e-mail in Rosaire's computer, whose password was Lumi's birth date.

Dear Rosaire,

Today, three mine employees disappeared. Sometimes I imagine us living in the South, in Montreal. I think about you, about sunny afternoons when we are all prisoners of the mine with just one desire: to escape and to see the blue, blue sky. One image haunts me: of you and me in a stone dungeon, imprisoned, making love. Trying to force each other's throats with our tongues, battling, almost, on our hands and knees, on the cell's gravelly floor, where a weak sound of water can be heard. Our love like a boxing match. I try to land blows on you so you will retreat, so that your head will strike the wall, before you come. Your love enrages me. Our love will never exist other than in fighting one against the other and against all others. And spitting in each others' faces. And, if it were possible, in killing one another.

But in the meantime, in my mind, I drag you by the hair. I drag you with my teeth over our imaginary corpses. Curled up in a corner, naked, in the light of a candle, we drink absinthe in porcelain cups that we light on fire. No cube of sugar, no pretty little steel spoons with a lace motif. We are in prison. Incarcerated. Our skin is covered in granular and bluish clay mixed with alcohol. Our hair is matted with sweat.

My visions of imprisonment make me want to starve myself, to feel the pain of being confined. The veins in my neck bulge as if from anger, beating against yours. My nails painted black dig into your flesh. Sharpen themselves in you. We fight to shake loose the love I bear within me, that it may vanish. So as no longer feel it well up. I want to strike you, to blacken your eyes so as no longer to love you. To hit you and to break this spell. I refuse to grovel any more within myself at the very thought of your being there.

On my desk, a little calendar with Inuit sculptures has on its September page the engraving of a caribou being attacked at the throat by two wolves. I look at it often. It's the only thing that calms me, this little image of a bloody assault. Otherwise, I plunge back into the captivities I invent for us so as to no longer love you, because I know that in your life I will never be the only one.

And so, on those beautiful afternoons we spend together, I want to make you drink alcohol. So that you will sink into hell. So that you'll become weak. I want you to submit to my blows in the hope of achieving orgasm. I want to endure, along with you, lacerations, throat slitting, asphyxiation. So as never more to love you, I will bring with me a pair of scissors to make little incisions in your skin. My wish is to kill you.

Marcelline

I had trouble understanding what it all meant. I had a headache and three days' worth of bags under my eyes. My brother had once again managed to pin me to the ground. He had stripped me of all hope, all capacity for happiness. At that precise moment, I wished that I could ask him what had been most important in his eyes.

Once again, my brother the brilliant lawyer had reduced everything to nothing. I felt myself implode. My understanding of the entire universe had just been shaken. Nothing before had ever affected my view of the world to that degree. I replied to the officer that nothing in this delirium made sense to me. That I'd been in love with Marcelline from the first moment I saw her. That this letter definitely did not come from her. That Marcelline did not like men. And I hung up.

39

Music Alters the Taste of Wine

When someone dies, to our great surprise his private life is suddenly laid open to view. His bank balance and his credit card bills arrive in the mail. His e-mail box and the passwords scrawled in his agenda are accessible to us, as are all the files in his computer.

I spent the day combing through Rosaire's apartment. I hoped it would put things in perspective and help me to understand some things. Perhaps it would lead me to his murderer? I listened to the Samantha Fox disc in his CD player. I opened a bottle of red wine left on the counter. Marcelline had told me once that music alters the taste of wine. This one smelled of geraniums. I was like a thief emptying out all the drawers in search of something. In the second drawer of the desk I found a text written by Rosaire. You'd have thought it was the rough draft of a reader's letter to *Playboy*:

I have become friends with another girl at the brothel. She comes to eat with us once a week. She wears only coloured imitation leather shoes and likes to eat blue Mr. Freezes that stain her tongue. When she is there I feel like a voyeur because Marie-Perle only has on her yellow lace bra and the little panties I like so much. Soon I'll have to stick a label in them with her name on it, because everything's going to be mixed up together. I imagine that Marie-Perle planned my meeting with Lumi with the secret purpose of having fun with her on Saturday night. They have become friends. Sometimes I go to bed early and I listen to them together drinking Cava the colour of a partridge's eye. With me, Marie-Perle is unforgiving. She bawled me out the other day because I'd brought home the wrong brand of soy milk. She wants Natural Light vanilla and I'd brought her the plain. If she knew that milk costs fifteen dollars a bottle in Iqaluit, she'd stop complaining. I'm convinced that someday one of them is going to poison me. Every day I walk in the woods and I gather a little piece of a toxic mushroom that I swallow immediately without breathing. By absorbing small doses of poison, I immunize myself against a dose that could be fatal. If I weren't there, Marie-Perle and Lumi could live happily together. They would do the shopping hand in hand, prepare picnics that they would eat by the river and they'd kiss, sated, lying in the grass, before going to sleep. I feel as if I no longer exist. Sometimes we make love, me and Marie-Perle, on Saturday morning before we go shopping, when she's still a bit drunk. But we haven't kissed for two years. Lumi has become what holds us together. When she is there, I hear Marie-Perle laughing again with her unembarrassed laugh. Without Lumi, we would no longer be together.

I didn't know to whom this text was addressed. Rosaire liked women too much. He was ready to live through the worst situations just for them. I began to have the vague impression that he'd sunk into a nameless delirium. And that it had cost him his life. I returned to Iqaluit on May 14, after four days of absence, because it had become unbearable for me to stay away from where my brother had breathed his last breath. Compared to his, my life suddenly struck me as being extremely monastic.

40

Polynya

A polynya is an everlasting hole in the ice. A source of life and un-hoped-for nourishment in the Arctic winter. The opening is maintained by winds and currents and also by whales, who must rise to the surface every twenty minutes to breathe. They prevent the ice from closing over. Polar bears come to fish in these fertile holes during the darkest days of winter. At the end of the cold season, the thick skin of the belugas is gouged from their repeated clawing.

Mitsy Cooper was waiting for me at the Iqaluit airport when my plane from Montreal landed. She'd called the day before on my cell phone, telling me that she had news and that she wanted to see me. What she revealed brought me back to life. She was overwrought, she was trembling, and her words spilled out:

"We have to go to Pangnirtung. That's where we'll find out who killed your brother. The police aren't doing anything so I did my own research. Tommy's waiting for us on the landing strip with a plane."

"Tommy nearly killed me the other day when he left the controls to go and piss off the rear end, in full flight. Then he dumped a Japanese tourist on an iceberg. You really have confidence in him?"

But Mitsy insisted and we left immediately. Pangnirtung is a baby Nunavut. The village is a forty-five minute flight from Iqaluit, on a fiord so high that Tommy had to tightly manoeuvre to land near the ridged wall of ice. I murmured:

"My God Tommy, you're going to kill us for real this time!"

"Ah, you monotheists, why are you so scared of death? Give me the bottle of whiskey in the knapsack down at your feet," Tommy shouted, wrenching his wheel round as far as it would go.

We could see small aircraft on the tarmac, like a scattering of model planes in a playroom. This town has one thousand three hundred inhabitants, including hip-hop teens who wear their caps backwards, women in modern parkas and a population of elders, traditional hunters.

Mitsy, seated in the rear, was talking to me, but I heard nothing because of the earphones and the noise of the propellers.

"Your brother ate puffballs at his last meal, and they may have been poisoned. We're going to meet the man who gave him the mushrooms. He lives in Pangnirtung. Puffballs have hallucinatory properties, and are used by the Inuit for divination. According to my sources, they're also eaten by some Whites in the neighbourhood..."

"That sounds much too romantic for me. Are you sure you aren't making this up for the scandal sheets? Your reference to a 'pink fix' was already, for me, over the top. It was pointless to slander him that way. My brother was a man respected in the community. He did everything he could to give the Inuit people territorial recognition."

When the plane landed, an Inuit in snow glasses and a leather jacket with the image of a spear-wielding hunter in relief, was waiting for us in front of a corrugated iron hangar. He seemed uneasy. The Pangnirtung community was preparing a commemorative ceremony to pay homage to a young man, originally from the village, who had jumped from a plane the previous week. On the wooden cross made for him, his father had plastered a Montreal Canadiens sticker. It was said that he had researched suicide on the Internet. The investigators had found the information in his computer's memory. According to the doctors, he suffered from *perlerorneq*, a depressive syndrome caused by winter darkness.

The man Mitsy wanted to meet was one of twelve sons of a dissident Inuit chief. He secretly detested the white man, the administrative authority in the North. He was an Inuit rights activist. His favourite pastime was to attack animal rights activists from Greenpeace.

"He targeted your brother for years," Mitsy told me. "He blamed him for his weakness in the negotiations on the autonomy of Nunavut. The

Inuit own the lands, but they have no rights to the exploitation of the subsoil. He saw that as abusive. He held your brother responsible for the current situation."

The man we wanted to meet seemed not to be around for the time being. And so we spent the night with the deputy mayor. That evening I thought about Marcelline a lot. Why had she yielded to Tommy? Did she love Rosaire? For her, I would have thrown up barricades against all those men whose only gift is to seduce women. They know how to spark love in them instantly, to satisfy them for a night. Against all who possess this talent, against this species that squanders souls with its age-old magnetism, I wanted to fight.

That night we ate muktuk and a village elder recited the legend of the solitary walker.

A Russian servant in Vancouver was still in love with the city of her birth and in 1927 she decided to go back to Vladivostok. She was very poor however, and could not pay for passage on a boat. She set off on foot. Her plan was to arrive at the roof of the world, because she imagined she could walk across the Bering Strait to Siberia. That is how she found herself at Hazelton in northern British Columbia in September, 1927. The first snowstorms had already started to blow through the region, and to protect her, the local chief of police put her in prison. But this winter behind bars did not lessen her desire to see Vladivostok again. When summer came, she continued to follow the telegraph line towards the north. Her journey had already become legendary. A telegraph company employee gave her a dog, for the road. When things got hard, she carried it in her arms to spare its paws, and when it died, she had it stuffed in rudimentary fashion and continued to drag it along with her. In the winter of 1928, she was found in Dawson City, working as a cook in a camp. She left in the spring. When asked where she was going, she just replied:

"To Siberia."

In August she arrived in Nome, Alaska. She was travelling sixty kilometres a day. She was only two hundred kilometres from the Bering Strait, almost in Russia. She left Nome pulling a sled. Then she disappeared. Her sled was found some thirty-five kilometres from Nome.

Polynya

It was refreshing to listen to him, because most of the people we questioned wanted money in exchange for their answers. Many people felt wronged by the Whites. One man suddenly raised himself up and cried:

"They're going to have to walk over the bodies of our ancestors and our own bodies before they open new mines in Nunavut. Legal and political strategies are no longer going to be enough for us."

The next day, Saturday, May 15, we visited the Canadian Army military barracks, where no fewer than five soldiers asked me for news of the beautiful Lumi. On the small bookshelf in their recreation room were the following volumes: *The New Father: A Dad's Guide to the First Year*, by Armin A. Brott; *My Secret Garden: Women's Sexual Fantasies*, by Nancy Friday; and the classic *Men are from Mars, Women are from Venus*, by John Gray. At the Inuit Coop in Pangnirtung, I saw that it was possible to buy Clamato, a mixture of tomato and clam juice, or nylon stockings for twenty dollars, some pale celery with no vitamins, wrapped in cellophane, for ten dollars, and a vast selection of coloured fishing lures at astronomical prices. Teens took their time trolling the aisles.

It was then that I saw on the shelf for goods on consignment, my brother's gold reliquary. I tried to stay calm. It was more and more obvious that Rosaire's murderer lived in this village.

"Who does this object in the shape of a finger belong to?" I asked the cashier, as I bought a box of After Eight for fifteen dollars.

"To a man who's not from here, but who lives on the new road built by the soldiers, near the bay. He also left a statue of the Virgin Mary on consignment, but people at the Iqaluit airport museum bought it yesterday," he answered, proudly.

He thought he'd made a good bargain and looked for us to agree as he closed his cash drawer. My head swam. Was this my ancestor's famous pietà?

Mitsy immediately rented two four-by-fours, and we went looking for the individual. The road was impassable. The wind was so strong that it threatened to flip the vehicles. We had to turn back.

We had been in Pangnirtung for three days when the man we sought went back to the Coop to see if the reliquary had found a taker. The police were waiting and tipped us off. To my great surprise, it was Kujjuk. Kujjuk, my dishwasher, with his aviator glasses and his missing arm. When I threw myself on him, taking him by the collar of his blue-and-black checked brushed cotton shirt, he tried to pierce my side with the hook on his prosthesis. The police pulled us apart. I was panting, I wanted to bite him in the face. To rip off his ears with my teeth.

"Where did you find that object?" asked one of the officers.

"It's a girl who came to see the soldiers once a month that gave it to me."

"Lumi?" I ventured.

"Yes, her."

"But Lumi hasn't been in Pangnirtung since March. That was well before Rosaire's death. Tommy can confirm it," I added, furious.

Again I lunged at him. But the police kept him away from me.

"Let me go, I didn't do anything," he protested.

"Kujjuk, we found a peach pit at the crime scene the day of Rosaire's death. We'll know from a DNA analysis if it's yours," said one of the officers.

A few months earlier, Kujjuk had developed a persecution complex. He thought himself more intelligent and upright than everyone else, and began to hate Rosaire. He thought it was unfair that a White so crafty and greedy, a foreigner born in the South, should in the name of his people assume control of the Lomonosov Ridge question. And so he'd done everything possible to find his weak point. Over the winter, spending his free days at Iqaluit and whiling away his evenings at the Arctic Circle bar, he got close to Rosaire. And one night he took action. He offered Rosaire bear liver with puffballs, claiming that it was a Pangnirtung specialty. He knew that the Whites had a weakness for Nordic gastronomical delicacies. Rosaire was drunk that Sunday. He'd arrived from Santo Domingo, where he'd spent a week. Kujjuk dared him to eat the raw bear liver, saying he wouldn't be able to. Without hesitating for a moment, Rosaire downed it greedily, before attacking the puffballs sautéed in butter.

Few people know that polar bear meat is not edible. Some explorers ingested it at times, but their reaction was always the same: they thought that the bear's avenging spirit was trying to kill them. Their skin and hair started to drop off. The Vitamin A found in toxic quantities in bear liver can cause hypervitaminosis.

Kujjuk finally confessed that he'd wanted to teach Rosaire a lesson, not to kill him. "It was an accident," he repeated. "I'm not a murderer. You're the guilty ones. You stole our culture, our land, our women."

At last I could breathe.

41

The Eunuch

The stolen pieta was well displayed in the Iqaluit airport's main hall, beside a seal sculpture in soapstone and a pair of snow goggles from the 1950s. The night we got back to Iqaluit, when no flight was scheduled for some hours because of bad weather, I went up to the sculpture and heard the voice of my brother.

The wooden statue had been repainted several times, in different colours. Under the base was inscribed, in blue ink, "The Chinese discovered America." It was definitely Rosaire's handwriting. I suddenly realized that the sculpture was light not because it carried God's message, but because it was hollow. Inside it I found, rolled up, Admiral Zheng He's Chinese map. It had been hidden in the Virgin's innards, and had travelled from church to church for centuries, surviving the worst disasters. Now I held it in my hands. It was my brother's final legacy and I would never be parted from it. I went back home with the map, not revealing anything. No one but Rosaire knew of its existence. The eunuch admiral's map, which had made the first circumnavigation of the earth at the beginning of the fifteenth century, would remain our last secret. Our bond would endure beyond death.

42

Bombus Polaris

They did not exchange rings. Tommy gave her his caribou tooth necklace, which she has worn ever since. She offered him a very ancient nautical ephemeris. This document, published annually for sailors by the Board of Longitudes, makes astronomical navigation possible. The flyleaf was inscribed with golden moons and planets with rings. It said: "My dearest memories are with you, Marcelline."

After her marriage to Tommy she tried to set up beehives behind her greenhouse in Kimmirut, an amateur apiary. The Arctic bees are called *Bombus polaris*. In Egyptian mythology, the role of bees is to choose the gods' elect, or the gods themselves. To placate them, the Egyptians offered the gods entire hives. In Greek mythology, honey was the principal foodstuff for Olympian meals, and that pleased Marcelline enormously.

Although married, Marcelline thought often of the only man who had seen into her heart. At night, she heard him in her dreams, and sometimes she even wrote him letters that she tore up at dawn.

In my heart you are like a priest, dressed in white, and silent. Love seeps from your skin. You say nothing. You remain imbued with this silence. Words not to be spoken. You look at me with the gaze of a wild beast, a murderer. A gaze that could so easily usurp everything. Clear dangers lurk in the pupil of your eye. Desires that could impede my growth. Turn me to bone. Have me die in childhood. I try to survive that terrible assault.

Polynya

I want you to give me something. I want you to say, of your own free will, without my asking it: "You are the only one in the world. I am overwhelmed. I am there. I am what you seek." I want you to go down on your knees to say it, I want you to swallow poison to make me understand that without me, you no longer want to be there. I want to exist in you. I want to devour your heart, to have your perineum melt away. I want to be the cause of your incurable disease. I want to make you tremble. I want you to kneel down before me. I want you to see my hair shining in the sunlight.

You have found your way, not too far from your home but too near for me to seek you out. If I had stayed, I would have been afraid every day. Afraid of you, afraid of myself, afraid of the future. Every day I would have been afraid, every day would have been filled with striving. Every day I would have read books and scientific journals to impress you. I would have wanted to inscribe myself in your genealogy. But I preferred a simple life. Comfortable.

43

Faro a Colomb

Tommy told me later that Marcelline often reread the postcard I'd sent her from Santo Domingo. She had slipped it into the slot of a kitchen cabinet, above the counter where she chopped vegetables. On a cork board beside it was pinned a plastic bag containing her grandmother's dried rose petals. Once, Tommy surprised her cutting a kiwi into the shape of a rose. She wept sometimes, when she took my card in her hands. I had chosen to let her go, to distance myself from her. It was the best way to show her my love.

Santo Domingo, January 11, 2011

Dear Marcelline,

In fishing you summon the fish that has isolated itself from the school, écarté, or set aside. I often feel like those who go their own way outside the herd. I'm not going to return soon, because I have chosen to live on the edge of a caldera not far from Santo Domingo. I am on Rosaire's trail. Here there are flights of pink flamingos, and I often swim in the company of three manta rays. Every morning, I eat a brazo de reina, literally a "queen's arm," a tamale that is a specialty of the region.

I've rented a little pink hacienda. The streets of my village are sand. People walk barefoot but they dance at bus stops and in the street. The restaurants and cafés are lit with candles and you can hear musicians playing melancholy chords all night long. At Santo Domingo I visited Columbus's lighthouse, a mausoleum that some say contains the ashes of Christopher Columbus. My first outing at sea was so miraculous that the fisherman made a sign of the cross when he set his foot on land. I don't miss eating arctic char. But I miss you. Since I no longer have a brother, I am seeking a family everywhere I am.

Ambroise

Acknowledgments

Thank you to Alexandra Linge, my first reader, to Mathieu for his impeccable memory and his stories of Baffin Island, to Marc-André, my favourite motivator, and to Gilbert, who taught me the meaning of the word perseverance. I would also like to thank the Canada Council for the Arts and the Conseil des arts et des lettres du Québec for their support.

About the Translators

Sheila Fischman is the award-winning translator of nearly 200 contemporary novels from Quebec. She·lives in Montreal.

Donald Winkler is a Montreal-based literary translator. He is a three-time winner of the Canada Council's Governor General's Award for French to English translation.